I0819790

Biblical quotations taken from the KJV, unless otherwise marked as ESV or NIV.

First Printing, 2021

A Missionary's Story

A Missionary's Story

A NOVEL

A.L. Helland

Willamina Studios

CONTENTS

I'd like to dedicate this book to all the Marilyns who know they aren't perfect but "seek the Lord and his strength; seek his presence continually," (Psalm 105:4 ESV) all the Davids who aim to "not grow weary of doing good, for in due season we will reap, if we do not give up," (Galatians 6:9) and to all the missionaries on and off the mission field.

ACKNOWLEDGMENTS

Mom told me to publish this book for years, but I procrastinated.

"I'm not old enough to publish a good book," I said. Then through a series of providential accidents, I published *Alchemist of Eternity*, a story I originally wrote as an experiment. The enthusiastic response I got was startling.

"I need more support," I said. Now with Willamina Studios, I'm surrounded by some pretty amazing people who have generously given a lot of their effort, time, money and prayers.

"The story is set in Colombia. I've never been there. I can't publish a book with inaccuracies," I said. Unknown to me, my proofreader, Joan Scofield, had been involved with mission work in Colombia. She pointed out any ignorance and approved my more accurate research. She even let me read some of her own stories from her time there, and showed me her souvenirs.

Long story short, if you're reading this, it means I finally did what I should've done all along and listened to my mother.

I wrote the first draft of this story in a pink notebook that probably wasn't mine while waiting for my sister to finish her violin lessons; I wrote the final draft many years later on my own computer with a proofreader waiting to check it, a company waiting to publish it, and an audience ready to read it. I'd like to thank my brother Daniel, for showing me continually as we grew up that the things we wanted to do, could be done. I'd like to thank Joan Scofield for fine-tuning this story. And most importantly, I'd like to acknowledge God's providence. He told Jeremiah "If thou return, then will I bring thee again, and thou shalt stand before me," or in another translation, "If you repent, I will restore you that you may serve me"

(Jeremiah 15:19a NIV). Repentance, returning, surrender... God starts us there, and brings us into restoration, and service to him. I'm learning how important and fulfilling that is. It's a big part of Marilyn's journey in *A Missionary's Story*. This book is fictional, but I think you'll find some very real truths woven into it.

In His Grip,
A.L. Helland
October, 2021

1

Footsteps South

On a chilly winter morning I stood in the living room, holding a coin in my hand. I rubbed it with my thumb absentmindedly, contemplating the words written on it. *United States of America, One Dime.* Ten cents weren't very important, but I knew this dime held sentimental value. As I put it down onto the coffee table, David's voice caught my attention.

"I want to show you something." He grabbed my hand and pulled me across the room. I nimbly hopped over the boxes and bags littering the floor. I knew each parcel contained old memories for David and his family: memories of another time, another place, another world. Letting go of me, he laid both hands on a small wooden crate, roughly built. "Ma says that this is the box my Dad's friend Misael made him. He kept it beside his bed. I want to show you something I found."

I watched as David's fingers pried up the lid. The hinges were old and rusty. When he had it open, he reached in, and slowly pulled something out, wrapped in a soft, light blue cloth.

"Is that a baby blanket?" I asked, touching the pretty fabric.

"Hmm? Oh, I don't know what that is. Some old rag or something." David carefully laid the bundle on the ground, and with a reverent air unwrapped an old, black book. He looked up at me, his blue eyes shining. "See?"

I nodded. "Yes, I see it. What is it?"

"It's my father's Bible," David replied, opening the front cover and flipping through the soiled pages. As I listened to the rustling of the book's leaves, I thought of David's father, whom I had never met.

Weldon Cole had been born an adventurer. During his life he had sought out dangerous locations and thrived in them. But what he had loved even more than exploration was the Bible, and God's calling in his life. In response to both passions, he, his wife Olivia and daughter Linda had moved to South America to bring the Gospel to jungle tribes. His second child, David, was born on the mission field. But after only a few short years, Weldon passed away, and his family returned to the States.

David's voice brought me back to the present. "Marilyn, look at this verse he wrote on the first page." My eyes scanned the open book, and finally rested on sloppy handwriting. All the letters seemed to be falling in different directions, he had capitalized every *W*, and several letters were backwards.

"For whether we live, we live unto the Lord; and whether we die, we die unto the Lord: whether we live therefore, or die, we are the Lord's."

David's bright eyes turned away from the page and looked up at me. "Marilyn," he whispered, "I wish you'd known my dad. He was... amazing."

I nodded, absently chewing on my fingernail, deep in thought. Weldon Cole had lived and died for Jesus, in a strange, foreign country, far away from home. It took an extreme amount of faith for a family to be on the mission field. The Coles had had that faith – Weldon, Olivia, Linda. And now, I knew David wanted it. Not only did he want to grow in faith, but he also wanted to follow in his dad's footsteps; footsteps leading south, far south, away from home. A sudden question struck me. Did I really have that kind of faith?

I turned my thoughts away from these deep musings and glanced about the living room of Olivia's house – at the grey walls, the white trim, and the ticking clock on the mantel. David and I had come to look through Weldon's things, searching for inspiration for our planned move. Reading the man's journal, digging through his clothes, investigating his home-made insect traps... it all brought us a step closer to our destination.

My name is Marilyn Cole. I was born in Washington State, to my wonderful parents John and Jenny Turner. In hindsight, I can see my desire to share the Gospel began early on in my life. I remember joining a street preaching club, as well as helping run a women's Bible study and volunteering at a children's summer camp. Not until I met David Cole did I ever imagine telling the story to people in a foreign land.

David Cole came into my life when I was seventeen years old; we married two short years later. I still remember the first time the dark-haired boy with bright blue eyes walked into the church my family attended, along with the rest of his family. His mother, Olivia Cole, was a quiet, gentle woman, with the laid-back and sweet nature that in many ways characterized her son. David's sister Linda, on the other hand, had all her father's drive and spirit.

David was the perfect balance between his parents, I think. Though easy-going, he was always going forward, driven by a mildly adventurous nature, but mostly his constant determination to fulfill whatever duty lay in front of him.

Six years after we had met, we were living down the road from my parents in a small mobile home, with our two children. Up to this time, we had both always felt the calling. There was no finger writing on the wall; just a small voice inside, telling us that sharing the Gospel was our life mission. But now, in 1972, the voice changed its message.

It no longer whispered, but instead we felt God telling us it was time to put our calling into action.

We talked about it. We prayed. And now we were both at peace with each other and God as to what we would now devote our lives to. Although it would be nearly two years before we finally reached the mission field, the pieces began falling into place almost immediately after our decision.

His sister Linda, who was now part of a national association funded by churches called the MLA, immediately began helping us get the wheels turning. Our family was approved by the board of directors, and David was scheduled to attend a linguist camp they held in Colorado.

The most difficult part for me in this process was explaining our decision to my family. It was one of the first things I did, just a few weeks after we found I was pregnant with our third child. It was a frosty day in late '72 when I walked into my parents' house to break the news. I had chosen a Sunday afternoon, knowing my two siblings would be home.

"Mom? Dad?" I called, my voice echoing through the silent house. A few hours earlier at church I had forewarned them of my visit. After a couple moments of empty hush, my younger sister poked her head into the room.

"Hello, Marilyn," she greeted, tucking a strand of her straight brown hair behind her ear. "We've been waiting and waiting for you, wondering what your announcement is!"

"Really?" I followed her down the hallway. "I mean, it's not that big of a deal..."

"Oh good!" she breathed a sigh of relief. "We've been imagining all afternoon what it could be! Dad said he had the feeling it was something big. Mom felt it was something bad. Steven said he had a few ideas, but he wouldn't tell us. But if it's not a big deal, whatever it is, then I suppose we've wasted the past few hours."

Knowing my family, I figured they had probably wasted the hours either way, but I made no note of that aloud. "Where are Mom and Dad?"

"Talking and guessing in their room. They'll be relieved when you tell them it's nothing important at all."

I sighed. I hadn't meant to give that impression; but it was too late. I made up my mind to tell them straight and avoid any beating around the bush. My mind drifted into other channels; had the kids woken from their naps yet? If they had, I hoped my forgetful husband remembered them.

"There you are!" my mother's shrill, shaky voice awakened me from my musings. "What's going on?"

As she spoke, she laid hold of my hand and led me through the doorway, with Meredith trailing behind. My eyes glanced swiftly about the room, taking in the familiar surroundings. My father was seated in his cozy easy chair, and Steven was on a red wooden three-legged stool. They both rose as we entered.

"What's up, sis?" my older brother Steven went right to the point. "You sounded awful mysterious at church today."

"I... I didn't mean to," I stuttered, my courage faltering under my family's critical stares.

"She says it's nothing important at all," Meredith announced reassuringly. I sighed in annoyance, and my mother sighed in relief.

"I knew it was nothing," she laughed, shakily, dabbing her eyes with a blue cloth. "I don't know why you all were so worried... chronic illness, the stock market, breaking up with David... all nonsense."

"I didn't come up with any of those silly ideas," Steven objected.

"Neither did I," growled my father, reseating himself and slouching back.

"Oh!" my mother squeaked.

"Well, Marilyn, what is it?" questioned my brother, reseating himself on the red stool. "Let's see if any of *my* assumptions are correct."

"Yes, tell us the news," Meredith said excitedly, plopping down on my parent's bed, which was covered with a beautiful blue and white quilt. My mother stood beside me, waiting expectantly.

"Well," I began uncertainly, "I don't know how to tell you this..."

"Open your mouth and spit it out," my father grumbled. "It isn't that hard."

My eyes turned towards him. This WW2 veteran had been nothing but good to me my whole life, despite his grouchy attitude. We three children had always loved and respected John Turner, and had listened with admiration whenever he recounted his exploits in Europe. Now, he was drumming his fingers on the windowsill, his brows furrowed impatiently.

"Well, what is it?" my mother abruptly interrupted my thoughts. On an impulse, I decided to blurt it out.

"David is going to Colorado next year to train as a linguist," I announced bravely, but then quickly shut my eyes and held my breath, waiting for the reaction. The room was silent for a few moments. *They're stunned,* I moaned inaudibly. *They are not pleased at all!* After waiting a few seconds for someone to speak, I slowly exhaled and cracked open an eyelid. My family was staring at me, with lopsided mouths and question marks in their eyes.

My mother cleared her throat. "What, exactly, *is* a linguist?"

I sighed, irritated.

"A linguist is someone who learns multiple languages, and understands the different dialect grammars," my brother spoke up. "But I can't imagine David as one. We don't understand what you mean, Marilyn. Please explain yourself."

"Why would David want to be a linguist?" Meredith was treading the line between baffled and amused. "What good would that do him? Can't we leave linguist stuff for Greek historians?"

"Please, clarify," pleaded my mother, who was beginning to grow anxious again.

I opened my mouth, but then closed it, pressing my lips together tightly. This wasn't going as quickly (or smoothly) as I had hoped.

Suddenly my brother, who had been frowning in deep thought, seemed to catch on. He rubbed his chin, and fixed his stern eyes on me. "This has nothing to do with Weldon Cole, right, Marilyn?"

"I don't know what you mean by that," I replied defensively, which only seemed to prove his new assumption.

Slowly he rose to his feet and began pacing the room, his feet thumping in even rhythm. "Weldon Cole had impressive ideas, but he was obsessed with them – to the extreme. He went south, deserting his country when it was in turmoil, and endangering the lives of his family." His searching eyes scanned me over. "We all know how that story ends."

"He died," I returned bluntly. "I don't see how that relates to the present."

"I don't see how, either," he replied coldly.

My father seemed annoyed with the dragging conversation. "Quiet, boy, and Marilyn – out with it, child!"

"Alright, let me explain. Steven, let me talk," I glanced at him sternly, sensing he was about to speak. "Let me tell you what I mean. David is going to be training as a linguist. He is joining MLA – the Mission Linguist Association." I swallowed as I observed my mother's countenance fall. "I don't know all the details, but we'll be in Colorado for a while training and learning Spanish. And then we're heading to South America."

My last words seemed to echo. I knew they were being repeated in my parents' minds – South America. Father had a thoughtful frown on his face, and Mother was dabbing her eyes again.

Meredith broke the stillness. "How long does it usually take to learn Spanish?" It was merely a query to end the hollow silence. I didn't answer, but instead gazed at a hairline crack in the floor, trying to come up with excuses for leaving before they could say what they thought.

My brother, always searching for details, spoke up. "When are you going to Colorado? Will your children be learning Spanish? Will the MLA fund you? Where do they get the money?" After firing these questions, one after another, he finally ended with what he knew was closest to my heart. "And is this really what you want for your kids?"

I straightened up and put on a firm expression, while I inwardly scrambled for something to say. Although David and I had already talked through our desires for our children, I wasn't sure of how to explain it, and therefore stood silently, searching for the right way to explain my convictions.

"Come on, girl!" my father groaned impatiently, "fire away!"

I glanced about the room, looking for a reassuring smile, for someone who believed in me. I only wanted support and understanding. But all I perceived was my brother's stony eyes. He viewed my dream as folly. *Lord, help me,* I prayed mentally. And then, I spoke.

"As I said, I'm not confident on the details. But I know God is. It's like that saying: he doesn't call the prepared, he prepares the called. For now, all I know is that the MLA intends to send us to Colombia."

"Colombia!" my mother exclaimed with all her drama. "The very heart of a wicked continent! Where the roots of violence and evil lie!"

"And you want to raise your family there?" Meredith's eyes widened in horror.

"It's not that bad," I argued sensitively, protecting my husband's dream home. My family knew nothing about Colombia, anyway. "You are all exaggerating!"

Steven fixed his eyes on me. "Colombia... *I've* heard much about it." He sank back down onto his red stool, his eyes narrowing. "More than you have, it seems; I wrote a paper on it once in college. From what I remember, it produces and sells more illegal drugs than any other country. Drug cartels are plentiful, and deadly. Colombia is also home to the ruthless rubber barons. Besides all this, much of it is a jungle! Infested with insects, strange creatures, incurable diseases, and treacherous tribes. Colombia is reportedly the most violent country on the face of this earth." He leaned forward, almost tipping over his stool. "And David's father died there. And now David is bringing his wife and children south. He is foolishly following in his father's footsteps... footsteps leading to death."

I shuddered, but before I could respond, my father spoke. "Steven, leave the girl alone. She and David can make their own decision, which, of course, they and they alone are responsible for. I think the idea is as stupid as you do, but let's not scare her now, not on a Sunday! It's my day of rest, so my day of rest it shall be. Save all bickering for Monday."

"Steven won't even be here Monday," objected my mother.

"Yes, Father, let Steven talk," pleaded Meredith. "It shouldn't take long to convince Marilyn of her mistake."

"No!" my father's tone was stern; his mind was made up. "I shall have no unsettling arguments on Sunday. That's what God created the other six days of the week for, and Sunday's for recovery."

"I think I should go home now," I mumbled as I backed up, stretching my right hand behind me to grope for the doorknob.

"I think you should," agreed my pale-faced mother, as she lifted the blue cloth to her eyes again. "Please, Marilyn, reconsider. Ponder what your brother has told you. You must always think before you act. Reconsider."

I nodded numbly, and then shut the door shut behind me. I leaned against it for a moment, and then slowly let my breath out. Away from my family's influence, a smile crept over my face. David and I were going to live out our dream; it was almost unbelievable. No matter what Steven said, God was in control... even in Colombia.

2

True to the Call

The next year and a half were a whirlwind of preparation, training, and bidding farewell to friends and family, as well as welcoming our third child into our home. Since we were a young family with several children, the MLA had deemed it best to send a single linguist with us to help with the work. I had hoped for one of the kind young women David and I met in Colorado, but instead the board of directors chose a young man named Peter Futterman. We had never met him, as he had trained before us, and had already left for Bogotá.

In early 1974, our departure was on the calendar. Right when least expected, we found I was pregnant with our fourth. We had thought our family was complete, with three children aged five, three, and one. This new little life caught us off guard, but it didn't shake David's resolve. He had been born in South America, and he tried to convince me that this baby could be, too. I was not enthused with the idea of labor in the jungle.

"It won't be in the jungle," David's sister Linda assured me one day. She and I were talking at her mother's house; she was on the sofa and I was on the old rocking chair. "You and David will be staying with Anthony and Joyce Carter near Bogotá for a while for your last bit of training."

"But we'll be in La Inez before I'm due," I reminded her. La Inez was the village our family had been assigned to, and we had heard that it was far removed from civilization.

She stood up and laid her hand on my shoulder. "When you think the baby is coming soon, the pilot down there will fly you to the Carters. There are hospitals and doctors there, and you can stay as long as you want. You'll be fine."

I nodded, rocking back and forth slowly, my anxiety relieved somewhat. We wouldn't be cut off from the rest of the world; there would be airplanes and hospitals and even English-speaking people at my disposal. I tried to keep myself reminded of this as our plane left U.S. soil. We weren't leaving civilization behind completely.

In March of 1974, David and I stepped into Colombia, along with our three children – Sadie, Jimmy, and Dennis. We were met by Anthony Carter, who immediately whisked us off to the missionary compound near Bogotá. We would stay there until we had both mastered Spanish, attending a course at the University inside the city.

I clutched onto one-year-old Dennis tightly as Anthony's old truck rattled down the bumpy road a few miles outside of town. I was squashed beside the driver with Jimmy next to me, staring out the windshield with wide eyes. Beside him, David and Sadie were gazing out the hole where the window should've been, pointing out a man selling cocoa beans and a bright eyed and dark-skinned woman wearing silver jewelry.

I glanced at my husband. "Do you think any of the missionaries around here might've known your father?"

He shook his head. "Not near Bogotá. We lived a hundred miles away from here, and he died over twenty years ago."

I tried to imagine how Colombia must have looked twenty years before, but Anthony's voice interrupted my thoughts.

"We are here," he announced, shutting off the engine and turning in his seat to look at us. "You are all ready for some *comida,* and *agua,* eh?"

I smiled and nodded at him, proud to know what he meant. Anthony spoke Spanish fluently, and even when speaking English seemed to use a Spanish accent. But underneath his hat's brim and his skin's dark tan, two blue eyes twinkled, betraying his Northern nationality.

"We'd love some food," David returned in response to the man's query. He opened the truck door and swung Sadie out. "Anthony, how long have you lived here?"

"How old are you, *amigo*?"

"Twenty-six," David answered

"When I said *adiós* to the States, you were not yet born," Anthony answered. "Now I am nearly fifty, and still here."

"You run the compound, don't you?" I asked, helping Dennis out the truck. "And this place serves as home base to all the missionaries in the surrounding tribes, right?"

"Yes, the compound is *ventajoso* to the missionaries – it is good, and it is also vital." He began walking towards the closest building, a quaint house built with brick. "We are their connection to town, and to the States. Sometimes we send supplies from here. And the belongings you brought from the States will be transported here by truck, and we shall send it to your new home. For now, it is time to meet your new *amigos* and see your partner in translating." He pushed open the door and held it for us. Outside it had been mildly warm, and the temperature was the same in the building. It seemed as if we had entered a mix between a dining room, lounge and meeting area, for there was a table with benches on either side and a few chairs scattered about.

Several people were seated around the table, but immediately rose as we entered. A rosy-faced woman, with brown hair streaked with gray, came towards us with arms outstretched.

"A precious, precious family," she greeted warmly, wrapping Dennis and I both in a tight hug. Releasing us, she turned and embraced David, Sadie and Jimmy. "I am Joyce Carter. Welcome to our home."

A tall man stepped over with his hand extended towards David. His face was covered in a dark beard, and his eyes peered out of narrow slits. Grasping my husband's hand firmly, he introduced himself. "My name is Jim Warden. I've worked in La Inez for nearly ten years... I will get you started, finishing my work."

We would be translating the New Testament into the tribe's language, a long process that normally spanned years. For us, we would be finishing the work Jim Warden had begun. I wondered why he was leaving but kept my thoughts to myself. He probably was lonely, just him among an indigenous people.

Joyce Carter reached over and gently laid a hand on my stomach. "I was told you were expecting. Children are a blessing from the Lord... you are very blessed."

"It will be difficult raising children in the jungle," Jim Warden remarked, his keen eyes sweeping over my little ones.

"When God calls, he also makes a way," David returned. "And Marilyn will be able to focus mostly on them. The translating job is for me and my partner... whom I have not yet met." He glanced toward the last occupant of the room.

"*¡Caramba!* You do not know him?" Anthony exclaimed, grabbing David's shoulder with laughter in his eyes. "That is funny. I assumed you did and I was not going to introduce him. Peter, come shake hands with him."

As Peter Futterman stepped over to greet us, I was immediately struck with his youth. The next thing that caught my attention were his round eyeglasses, meticulously clean. His dark hair was neatly combed back, and I wondered if he spent more time on it than I did with mine.

"Good to meet you, Peter," David said, shaking the young man's hand heartily. "Have you been to La Inez yet?"

"No," Peter returned. "I haven't gone farther than Bogotá and this compound."

"Come, sit down," Joyce invited. "We were about to eat. I'll bring the food out."

After washing hands, I shuffled the little ones into seats. Peter laid a hand on Sadie's brown curls. "What is this angel's name?" he queried, smiling at her.

"I'm Sadie," she returned before I could answer. "Who are you?"

"I'm Peter," he replied, sitting down on a chair.

Anthony tapped his plate with his fork and the table hushed. Folding his hands together, he gave a short prayer in Spanish. I understood a couple of the words, but I couldn't catch the general meaning. I figured he was probably thanking God for the food and left it at that.

After everyone had tasted their first few bites, taking the edge off their hunger, a conversation started. Anthony led it, slipping back into his North American accent under the influence of our voices. He told of how years ago, only English was spoken on the compound. They even got the English edition of the newspaper. Unfortunately, it slowed down the progress of young missionaries who couldn't leave for their assigned villages until they had mastered Spanish. Therefore, they now spoke this language as often as possible.

Then he told of the jungle. His details of the rain, the foliage, the animals and the people riveted our attention and we asked countless questions. He recounted stories of snakes and tapirs, and told of insect bites and poisonous frogs. Here outside Bogotá, these things seemed very far away.

Sadie and Jimmy began nodding their heads, while Dennis was whining. Joyce showed me our room, and I immediately settled them into bed. I then returned to the main room where the others were still talking.

Joyce had cleared the dishes from the table, and the only things remaining on the surface were three lit candles. A lantern hung from the nearest wall, giving the room a golden glow. Outside, the sun had set, and the stars had ascended into their assigned places. I sat down beside David and laid my hand on his shoulder.

"David, Marilyn," Anthony began, "Let us talk about you now, eh? Do you feel called to this fearsome jungle?"

We both nodded. "God calls all His children to spread the Gospel," David said. "Some go abroad, some share the Good News through their ordinary lives. In the last chapter of Matthew Jesus says, 'Go ye therefore, and teach all nations, baptizing them in the name of the Father, and of the Son, and of the Holy Ghost: teaching them to observe all things whatsoever I have commanded you.' We're responding to that call."

"Hmm! And are you not frightened?"

"'Who shall separate us from the love of Christ? Shall tribulation, or distress, or persecution, or famine, or nakedness, or peril, or sword?'" I recited from Romans eight.

"'Neither death, nor life, nor angels, nor principalities, nor powers, nor things present, nor things to come, nor height, nor death, nor any other creature, shall be able to separate us from the love of God, which is in Christ Jesus our Lord,'" David finished.

Anthony smiled, his bright white teeth reflecting a candle's light. "Very good. You know your scripture."

"Why does the village of La Inez mean so much to you?" Joyce queried, joining in on the interrogation. "You have never seen it."

David laid a small New Testament onto the table. "When I want to hear the truth, I reach into my pocket. Sometimes we take the scriptures for granted. I can't imagine not being able to read for myself the words of Christ."

"La Inez already means so much to us," I said, warming up to the subject. Growing up, I had read the accounts of missionary wives such as Ann Judson, Henrietta Shuck, Elizabeth Dwight and Harriet Newell, and had learned the response to such statements. "Towns and cities, houses and luxuries are here today and gone tomorrow. Eternity will last forever. If we lived in the States, a hundred years from now our house may be crumbled or abandoned. But when we spread the Gospel, it creates a chain reaction that will never stop spreading until Jesus returns."

"Don't you think missionary work should be left for single men and women?" Jim Warden spoke up. Somehow, his question didn't sound as friendly as the Carters'. "Children should be raised at home and educated in school. They can serve as a distraction to the ministry."

"The family *is* the ministry," David said stubbornly. "Indigenous families need examples of Christian families. And we shouldn't act like foreign school teachers, either, doing everything for them. They need to see an example to follow, from a father, mother, and children, living in harmony with each other and God's Word."

Anthony nodded. "In theory, I would agree. This is not a world of only singles... God's family while on this earth is not one of only singles. All of us can be represented on mission fields. Children are a blessing, even in the jungle."

Jim Warden still didn't seem convinced. "I once saw a missionary family in Ecuador," he recalled. "They were a disaster. The parents were distracted with their children, putting them first, before the people of the tribe. They accomplished nothing; only wasted a lot of time and funds."

"I would say the Christian family is essential," Anthony said. "If we want to show these people a higher standard of living, what better way is there than to live it? There is a large place for single missionaries – Peter, for example. Our good friend Kara Perry also was a single missionary in Guatemala before meeting Jake and moving out here. God is the one who gives the calling, but He is also the one who gives the children."

"I was a missionary kid," David reminisced. "I was born in this country, but I didn't distract my parents. Their focus was clear; to raise a godly family, and to spread the Gospel to those who don't know it."

Jim Warden didn't respond. Anthony was in deep thought, and a general hush seemed to settle over the table. My brother Steven's eerie words suddenly returned to mind. *Footsteps... footsteps leading to death.* Was that the trail David and I were leading our family down? I laid a hand over my stomach and shuddered. I felt David's arm wrap around my shoulders and I felt reassured. God had us all safe within His hand.

3

In Bogotá

Late the next morning, I awoke to the sound of David crawling out of bed. He was looking out the window, so I quickly joined him, and something immediately caught my attention.

An orange Piper Cruiser plane was landing on the compound's runway. Several bright-eyed Colombians were dancing around in excitement, watching it land. I quickly became as enraptured as them.

The pilot was putting on a show for his audience down below. Shooting upwards, he dropped again suddenly, nosediving towards the runway, and it looked as if he had lost control. I recognized it as a stunt I'd seen at an airshow. The Colombians turned and fled, glancing over their shoulders with terrified expressions. The Cruiser pointed up again just before hitting the ground and circled high above their heads. It finally completed a beautiful landing, rolling to a stop near a tin shed.

David pulled on his clothes and ran out to greet the pilot. Before I could escape, Dennis woke up. I quickly scooped him up and brought him with me. As I passed through the front room, Joyce was cleaning the table. "I am sorry you missed breakfast," she said with a smile, "But I have kept yours warm."

"Thank you," I returned. I was a little disappointed about missing the breakfast conversation with Anthony, Peter, and Jim Warden, but I pushed it out of my mind. "Who landed out there? Is that the compound's airplane?"

She shook her head. "That is Jake Perry," she answered. "He's the bush pilot. He lives in one of the villages, and flies supplies to the others."

"Is there an airstrip at La Inez?"

"Fortunately, yes," she returned. "When Jim Warden arrived, that is when they built the airstrip."

I shifted Dennis to my other arm. "I'm going to join David outside."

She nodded. "Go ahead. Jake will be glad to meet you."

I slipped out the front door into the thin, chilly air. The fair-haired pilot was leaning against his airplane, talking with my husband. The aircraft was about twenty feet long with a wingspan of maybe thirty feet. The frames of the wings were aluminum, covered with fabric. It looked as if it could fit the pilot and a few passengers comfortably.

"This is my wife, Marilyn," David introduced me as I walked up. "And our son, Dennis."

The pilot nodded and smiled. "Hallo, ma'am." His voice was slightly higher pitched, but what I noticed was the harsh German accent which I had so often heard my father mimic.

"You must be Jake Perry," I answered, returning the smile.

He nodded. "I'm the mission pilot. We did have another airplane and pilot, but both were recently... put out."

My eyebrows furrowed slightly. "Was there a crash?"

"Yes. Kevin is in America now, and I'm not sure if he's coming back. The airplane is still sitting in the tree it landed in." A wry smile covered his face. "Here, the trees are so close together sometimes it's hard to get places."

I nodded understandingly, but inside wondered if he was referring to them recovering the craft or the airplane itself on its last trip. "Do you hail from the States?" I wasn't sure why I asked. For some reason, I couldn't stop thinking about my father's stories from the '40s.

"Yes," he replied. "My parents came from Germany, but I was born in the U.S."

I nodded again, wondering if his father had been around to watch his nation destroy countries, cities, and lives. I quickly turned my thoughts away. "How fast can this thing go?"

Jake's blue eyes glanced towards his craft. "Oh, maybe one-forty miles an hour."

"I suppose you're always buying fuel for it."

He nodded. "I'll put thirty gallons in her, and that'll hold her for a while, but it seems we're always ordering more. Anthony and I have gotten all the good deals figured out though."

We chatted for a little while about his plane. The mission compound and runway were situated in the hills just outside Bogotá. In a way, it reminded me of the countryside in the States. There was an assortment of birds wandering around, scratching the dirt; chickens, geese, and others that I couldn't remember the names of. A large garden was spread out behind the shed, and a couple of hired hands were busily occupied in it. It was a happy little place; the Colombians lounging about were mostly farmers or workers from nearby, and many of them were converts.

One of the audience who had watched Jake's show suddenly ran up to us, speaking rapidly in Spanish. David and I glanced at each other. We had studied the language for quite a while, and yet it was a struggle to make sense of what the man was saying. Jake smiled and shook his head, replying with a couple words. The man seemed disappointed but didn't leave. Instead, he glanced at David and me and said something more.

"What was he asking?" David asked.

"He was wondering if I needed help with the Cruiser, but I told him no. Now he's wondering who you two are. Alejandro, you know English; ask them yourself."

"Who are you?" Alejandro asked immediately, his eyes glittering with curiosity.

"My name is David Cole, and this is my wife Marilyn. We're here to learn more Spanish, and then translate the Bible in La Inez."

"*¡Guau!* That is very good. La Inez needs Bible. I've never been there, but I know it does." He grabbed David's hand and squeezed it warmly. "I am Alejandro. Dr. Culbert will teach you new language; when you are not at the University, I will be helping you remember Spanish. We will learn very fast."

David returned the squeeze. "Glad to meet you, Alejandro. I hope we'll learn fast."

"I'd better fill up the tank," Jake said, straightening up and heading towards the shed. "Alejandro, ask Joyce if she could fix me a meal. I haven't eaten a bite since yesterday noon. My wife Kara hasn't been home; she's helping at one of the other villages. Several small children were attacked by a tapir."

Alejandro shook his head. "That is bad."

"I agree," Jake returned. "I stopped by there this morning. I think they'll be fine, but I hope they've learned their lesson. Don't frighten a two-fifty pound tapir at dusk!"

"Have you had time to eat yet?" Alejandro asked as we walked towards the Carter's house.

David shook his head. "But we weren't busy, like Jake," he admitted. "We got up late."

Alejandro smiled. "I have eaten, but I will eat again with you. So will Jake. We will have an *alegre* breakfast."

I was no longer upset about missing breakfast with the others. Alejandro and Jake were friendly people, even if my mind was still labelling them as the Colombian and the German, rather than letting them be themselves.

Ten minutes later, David and I were seated at the table with our three children. Jake and Alejandro sat with us, both shoving the eggs and fried peppers into their mouths as fast as possible. It was hard to tell which of the seemingly starving men had already eaten.

After the growlings in his stomach were silenced, Alejandro began to talk. "Anthony told me you were coming. He say you have three children and another coming." He glanced at me. "You are expecting?"

I swallowed my bite before replying. "Yes, the baby is due in July."

"Wonderful!" he exclaimed. "You will have the baby here, no?"

"Yes, either here or in Bogotá," I answered. "But we'll be in La Inez before then... as long as it doesn't take us until July to learn Spanish."

"It won't," Alejandro assured me. "When baby is coming, Jake will fly you back here?"

Jake set down his glass of water. "When Marilyn is ready, I'll fly her here. All they need to do is radio the compound and they'll send me her way."

So we still weren't leaving civilization behind entirely. When I needed it, we would use a radio to bring an airplane our direction. I smiled slightly, feeling glad that we weren't being stranded in a rainforest without any connection to the outside world.

"Where's Peter Futterman?" David asked as Joyce entered the room.

"He's with Anthony," she answered. "When you're done eating, you'll join them. Anthony will drive you to the University for the afternoon class. I will watch the children."

From that day forward, David, Peter and I went almost daily for vigorous Spanish lessons from Dr. Culbert. When we were at the compound, Alejandro would assist us, happily correcting our mistakes, which at first were plentiful. When we began to get a better feel for the language, Anthony insisted that we speak it more than English.

Our time at Bogotá was a time full of memories. We explored the modern town with Peter, roamed the markets with Alejandro as our guide, took an eight-hour trip in the back of a pickup to visit one of the nearest missionary families, and interacted with the people and their culture. The city had brick buildings, paved roads and cars, but was still distinctly different from the States.

Jimmy's toddler prattling turned into Spanish words. Sadie picked up on the language too, but couldn't seem to separate herself from English entirely, normally using a mix of the two to get her ideas across. I smiled every time I thought of us moving to La Inez. There, they had a completely different language not derived from Latin at all. Some of them could speak Spanish, which would help us connect with them and learn their own language.

One day while David and I were walking through town, waiting for Anthony to pick us up, we ran into Jim Warden. We hadn't seen him much since our arrival, as he had been in La Inez preparing to leave. Peter and Alejandro were both with us.

"Do you think you have a firm handle on Spanish?" Jim Warden asked.

David nodded, and proudly said in Spanish, "*Yo creo*. Anthony will rarely let us use English, which has helped. We'll be ready to move to La Inez soon."

Warden glanced at me, and continued in English. "Do you think it is prudent to move into the jungle, with a child on the way?"

"Nothing is more prudent than investing my life in eternity," I answered, and I was very proud of the way it sounded. "And the baby will be fine. Once we have met the people of La Inez and settled into our home, I'll return here for a while."

He shook his head. "That is such a distraction to the ministry of Christ."

I pressed my lips together and felt my anger rising. Before I could respond, David said, "It won't be a distraction. It will take Jake barely any time at all to fly her and the kids back to the compound. Please, sir, leave it to us, the Carters, and the MLA mission board to determine what is a distraction."

He shook his head gravely. "I fear you young people have come only for an adventure. You are focused on yourself, and not the cause of Christ. You have come for the mere novelty of it."

"That's not true," David objected. "We came because we love Jesus, and because we love the people of La Inez. We want to point them to the truth."

"You will not convince anybody of the truth," Jim Warden pushed. "You are too frivolous... you lack seriousness and sense. I haven't known you long, but I've seen enough young people to know you will act childish and give them shallow theology."

Alejandro tried to steer the conversation down calmer channels. "I saw Anthony's truck pass," he announced. "We must hurry to our meeting place."

"The people of La Inez need someone to point them to their sin," Warden continued, ignoring the Colombian. "They need to hear the truth: the whole truth, not watered-down scripture. They are a wicked people bound for Hell."

"I don't see how children will keep us from teaching the truth," David returned.

"I've told you before, and I'll tell you again. I have seen many young families in missions all over the world. They are distracted, they don't focus on what is true. They come for the thrill and drama of it and are driven by their emotions."

"Anthony will be growing impatient," Alejandro interjected in Spanish.

David had been opening his mouth to reply to Warden, but Alejandro's statement cut him short. He paused, but then said, "*Adiós*, Warden. I'm sorry if my family does not meet your standards, but it's God's standards we're concerned about. My father successfully spread the Gospel and raised a family, and I pray I can too."

Peter and Alejandro turned away, and David and I began to follow them. Warden suddenly grabbed David's arm, and I instinctively stopped as well. "I didn't want to mention this to you," Jim Warden said in a tight voice barely above a whisper, "But I knew your father."

David glanced back at him with a slight shrug, wondering what the grave impact was. Jim Warden didn't leave us confused for long.

"He isn't who you think he was. He brought trouble to his family and the village, and died a shameful death."

Using his other hand, David gently removed the man's grasp on his arm. "I'm sorry, sir, but my Ma has told me differently. Dad died from fever. *Adiós.*"

We tried to catch up with the other two, but Warden took hold of both of us. "He was murdered in a fight," he said in the same low tone. "Your father did not know what was good for him."

David wrenched himself away. "You've already dumped on my family enough; don't lie about my father."

"It's true," he answered. He didn't speak with a mean or angry tone, but his manner still terrified me. His cold fingers were still digging into my arm, but I was paralyzed and didn't attempt to get away. Suddenly, the man's eyes turned and met mine. "Do you believe me?"

Of course I didn't. Although I had never met him, I knew Weldon Cole from the countless stories from Olivia and Linda; but the man's serious manner still unnerved me. I jerked free and reached for David's hand. He put his arm around me, and I again felt the sense of assurance I always felt when he held me. I looked at Warden and replied, "I trust my husband. I don't know how you knew Weldon, but David and his mother are his family. They knew him."

"Ask Anthony," Jim Warden returned in a deathly serious voice. "He might know. Goodbye; go back to the compound, and to your silly little adventure. I pray God saves that tribe!"

David and I turned and ran away holding hands like two frightened children. We caught up with Peter and Alejandro just as they were turning the corner where Anthony was waiting. They glanced at us as we ran up panting but made no comment. They jumped into the back, while David and I sat in the cab.

"Anthony," David began as soon as the doors were safely closed, "Did you know my father? Weldon Cole?"

He shook his head and replied in Spanish. "I did not know him personally," he answered, "But I do know who he is."

"How did he die?" David asked, switching to the other language.

Anthony shook his head again. "I am not sure," he returned. "Most reports say he died from an illness, but I have heard differently. Only his family, and perhaps the Colombian government would know for sure." He glanced at us sideways. "Do you not know?"

"I know," he answered quickly. The rest of the drive home was spent in silence. I could tell by David's fidgeting that Warden's words were bothering him, but I didn't say anything to comfort or assure him. I felt uncomfortable myself.

When we finally rolled up to the mission compound, I opened the door before Anthony had even turned off the engine. David slid out behind me and we headed toward the Carters' house.

"David, Marilyn!" Peter called, jumping out of the back of the pickup. We paused and let him catch up. "Alejandro and I were wondering when the Spanish class ended. Do you know?"

"Sometime this month," I answered. "Joyce has the schedule, we can ask her."

"So, we'll be in La Inez soon!" David exclaimed brightly, obviously cheered up by the thought. He grabbed my shoulders and looked into my eyes. "Marilyn, can you believe it? We'll be real missionaries soon, telling the Good News to those who have never heard!"

"Not exactly," I answered. "The people of La Inez have already had a missionary living with them for years. I don't know if they've responded to it or not, but we can't take credit for bringing it to them first."

"*Español, amigos,*" Anthony said as he walked past.

David quickly switched to Spanish. "We'll still be real missionaries, Marilyn. I'm glad we'll be able to move into Jim Warden's house immediately; if we don't like it, I'll build you a new one, I promise."

Alejandro walked up to us. "Will you be leaving for La Inez very soon?"

"I think so," Peter answered. "Maybe this month."

"I will miss you," Alejandro said, "but I am glad that La Inez is getting the Bible. I have a Bible, in my language, but they do not."

4

Just Like Home

Several weeks later, we finished the Spanish course. Preparations immediately began to bring us to our new home. Since a missionary had already lived there several years, there wasn't too much anxiety, since we didn't have to worry about building a house or airstrip. Finally, in late June of 1974, Sadie, Dennis and I squeezed into Jake's airplane. David and Jimmy had flown out early that morning. We had our clothes, some bedding, a radio and a handful of cooking utensils among other necessities packed in the back. After an hour or so, our German pilot told us we were close.

Sadie and I peered out the windows; little Dennis was squeezed between us. Jake's wife Kara was sitting up front, as she had insisted on coming with us to help set up our new home. She was a medical nurse who had trained in a University back in the U.S., and had been married to the German for a couple years. Kara was bright eyed and lively, a perfect balance to Jake's laid-back personality.

"There it is," I breathed, pressing my forehead against the window to see better. The plane was dropping rapidly, and the trees below seemed to be rising up to meet us. I squinted my eyes and observed a strip of ground devoid of trees. It was shorter than the runway at the compound, and I began to worry about our landing. I tried to assure myself that Jake had made this landing before and was perfectly capable of doing it again. I suddenly thought of the other pilot Kevin, who landed in a tree and was now recovering in the States. I shuddered.

"This is La Inez," Jake announced, leisurely moving the controls and glancing back towards us.

Keep your eyes on the airstrip! I felt like screaming, but I kept my mouth shut. Jake began telling Kara something and I wanted to tell him to stop and focus. I pressed my lips together and silently prayed that God would remind that pilot he was flying. Jake finally stopped talking and completed the landing perfectly.

I glanced out the window as Jake turned off the engine. There were two buildings in sight, spaced far apart. One was obviously made by the people of the tribe, built with mud, wood and woven leaves for the roof. The other appeared to have sprung up with the help of foreign hands, as there were nails, straight wooden planks and other familiar material.

"Let's unload quickly," Jake said, turning in his seat to face us. "Somebody call David over. I'll refuel the plane, and then fly back for Peter, Warden and the rest of your things."

"While he's gone, we'll begin setting up your house," Kara explained, opening her door and sliding out. "We'll make it feel just like home."

I glanced at the unfamiliar foliage surrounding the small clearing and suddenly felt a strange rising in my stomach. This wasn't home. My heart began aching, and my mind began asking why I was here, far away from my real home. David had come over and was unloading our supplies, but I simply sat there. Sadie and Dennis clambered down and joined Jimmy, looking around excitedly, but I stayed in the seat.

Jake walked past the open door dragging a large can of fuel. Kara chattered with my kids and led them up to Jim Warden's house. David walked by briskly, holding as much luggage as he could carry. But I hardly noticed; I was no longer in Colombia. I was far away in my parent's room, listening to my older brother Steven.

"Jungle... infested with insects, strange creatures, incurable diseases, and treacherous tribes. Colombia is reportedly the most violent country on the face of this earth..." That's what Steven had said, but I hadn't listened. I was in a new world where nature was dangerous and people were dangerous. It wasn't solely fear that made me long for home; it was also the sense of abandonment. My family didn't want me here. Neither did my friends. Now who would be my family, and who would be my friends? Where *was* my true home? My source of happiness, love, comfort... where people accepted me the way I was, and honored and supported my decisions. Where was that place?

In the center of God's will, my mind told me – my brain, which I had filled with missionary stories, had taught scripture, and had grounded in truth. But my emotions cried out a different story. The feeling inside my heart told me that I was by myself, that I was now cut off from the loving world. I was out in the middle of nowhere, trying to continue a dream that Weldon Cole had started.

Jim Warden's words floated into my head. "He wasn't who you think he was... your father did not know what was good for him." What did that mean? Was Weldon, our hero, simply another foolish man longing for adventure and thrill? In twenty years, would people be saying the same thing about me?

"Marilyn, are you getting out?" Jake asked impatiently. His German accent reminded me again of home, mainly of my father, who had mimicked it fairly well in retellings of his scrapes with Nazi soldiers. I pushed thoughts of home out of my mind and alighted from the aircraft.

Several women and children were hovering at the edge of the clearing, watching us. I knew that Jim Warden had forewarned them of our coming, and I wondered where the men were. David shoved an armful of things into my arms and told me to bring it to the house. I approached the structure, which was built on poles above the ground. There were rough steps that led up to the small porch and the front door. I wondered why it hadn't been built flat on the ground.

After ascending the stairs and walking through the doorway, I got the first glance of our new home. There was a mud stove in the corner with a shelf beside it, and a single hammock on the other side. A lonely chair sat against the wall, while a wooden desk occupied another corner, covered with papers and books. There was a small bookshelf, barely any higher than Sadie, and that completed the furniture. I looked around desperately for a table, a dresser, or an actual bed, but no such sight met my searching eyes.

"This is cool, mama," Sadie chattered in Spanish. "I like this house. But I don't want to fall off the porch onto the ground."

Jimmy was trying to pull himself up into the hammock, but it swung over and dumped him headfirst out the other side. With his father's determined look in his eyes, he held back the tears and began to try again. Dennis was pushing the desk chair across the floor towards the stove with a mischievous expression on his face.

David pushed past me and dumped his load into the middle of the floor. "Jake's leaving now," he told me, grabbing Dennis before he was able to climb onto the chair. "He'll be back in a few hours with Pete and Warden. He's in a hurry since he can't fly in the dark. Then we'll have a couple days to settle into this place before the village men get back."

"Where are they?" I asked, slowly dropping the baggage I held onto the floor.

"The chief and several others are out hunting, but most of them are working for the rubber barons. Warden told me that they should all be back soon, though. Once we get to know their chief and their shaman, the whole tribe will accept us and we'll be good to go. Those are the two people we need to focus on."

I nodded automatically and helped Jimmy into the hammock. David walked out and several moments later, Kara entered. She began unpacking our things, setting our utensils and food supplies beside the stove, our blankets and clothes by the hammock, and our books and radio on the desk. I forgot that I should be helping her, and simply rocked Jimmy back and forth.

"Is something wrong?" her sweet voice suddenly asked. I glanced up and wondered how she'd known, not realizing that it showed very clearly on my face. I shrugged, and then sighed.

"Maybe I'm homesick. And David isn't paying any attention to me." I pulled up the chair and sank down into it. "I feel exhausted and I just don't want to be here."

She stood there silently for a moment before responding. "After a good night's sleep and some food, Marilyn, I think you'll feel better. Sometimes, when we begin to spiral like that, the best thing we can do is rest and eat. Remember the story of Elijah in the Bible? He had been through a lot and was in the middle of nowhere by himself having a pity party. God didn't reprimand him; He told him to rest and eat. Elijah was not alone, and neither are you."

"I feel stranded," I argued. "I feel like I made a terrible mistake and there's nothing I can do about it."

"Marilyn, our feelings aren't what's true. We may feel like God isn't in control, but the Bible says He is, and that's the truth, no matter what our feelings are. Our emotions sometimes hide who God really is. Our human minds sometimes miss His sovereignty." She smiled and picked up Dennis. "Let's get this house ready for your family, Peter and Jim Warden to sleep in tonight. We'll arrange the bedding and pillows on the floor for you, David and the kids, and string up hammocks for the men on the porch."

Kara kept me busy for the next several hours, sorting through our things and setting up the house in the most comfortable fashion possible. Outside, David was assembling a table and several little chairs from pieces we had brought with us from the compound.

At noon we stopped and ate the lunch we had brought on the front porch. I glanced around for some natives of La Inez, but everybody had disappeared. Kara told me that they had probably gone back to the yuca fields or their own homes.

Late that afternoon, the airplane buzzed into sight and landed on the airstrip. Jake, Peter and Jim Warden jumped out, and everybody helped carry the remaining baggage. I glanced around at all our earthly belongings, which were few compared to most homes in the States. We would have to adapt to the way of life the people of La Inez would show us.

Jake and Kara left to make it home before total darkness. From our village to theirs, it would take them around a half hour. We did a radio check, and my heart was soothed slightly to hear Anthony's voice coming to us from miles away. We still had communication with the outside world... we weren't removed from life and love yet. Jim Warden sat with David and Peter at the desk and began introducing them to the language of these people, these children of the jungle. He showed them his grammar charts and his lists of nouns and verbs, until the shadows outside began to grow.

I settled Sadie, Jimmy, and Dennis under their blankets, and then sat down beside them with my back against the rough wall. David lit a lantern, and I thought of the Carters. Even though they had electricity, they enjoyed lighting candles and lanterns. Here we had no electricity, and therefore had no choice.

The world outside was calling for our attention. The cicadas grew quiet after sunset, but I could hear the wings of large beetles begin to whir, and strange insects were chirping, bidding the moon goodnight. I heard something scurrying outside the wall, but was too tired to worry about whatever rodent it could be. Only a low, ominous growl aroused me from my sleepy condition.

"What was that?" I whispered. David, who was leaning over the desk studiously, lifted his head attentively. Peter glanced up as well, but Jim Warden seemed unconcerned.

"It's a jaguar you heard, probably," he said, stacking his papers. "Searching for food in the jungle. We built this house above the ground so the animals would walk *beneath* it, rather than *through* it. It won't bother us."

Although I knew we were safe, the thought of a wild animal licking his lips just a couple yards away was disconcerting. I pulled my knees up under my chin and glanced at the small, sleeping bodies beside me, and then sighed. All the excitement had slipped out of this missionary life. Now I was faced with reality; my children were sleeping on the floor, while a huge cat lurked outside.

Why am I here, God? I asked silently. I lifted my eyes toward the ceiling, almost hoping to see an angel descending with a reasonable answer and explanation. But instead, all I saw was a gigantic spider slowly dropping towards the ground on a silky strand. I don't normally scream; but I did then – and loudly.

David jumped up, overturning his chair, and stared at me with red, sleepy eyes. Peter turned in his seat and glanced around, quickly observing the cause of the disturbance. As he used a book to knock the spider out of its web and beat it to death, I turned to my awakened children and made them lie down again. Out of the corner of my eye, I could see Jim Warden looking at me, with the same expression of displeasure he had shown at the Carters' house. I tucked Sadie's blankets down again, my hands shaking with anger and frustration. Why was I here?

5

The Chief and the Shaman

The following morning I awoke to the distinct smell and feel of cold air. I sat up and glanced around, noting that my children were still sleeping. I felt the sensation of freshness, growing plants and the rising sun I had felt years before when camping with my family, and I realized our new home didn't offer much more sealed protection than the tent I had slept in as a child.

I scrambled to my feet and glanced toward the front door, wondering how much privacy it would give us. Keeping an eye on the large cracks in the wall between the planks, I quickly dressed myself, keeping quiet to avoid waking David or the children. When I was finished, I used the claws of one of Jim Warden's hammers I found on the floor to pry open one of our boxes. Knowing that the contents of the crate hadn't seen the world since it had been shipped from the States made it a somewhat special task.

With the lid off, I dug through it until I found a small mirror. I propped it up on the desk and began fixing my hair. I suddenly thought of Jim Warden, and prayed he wasn't awake, and if he was that he didn't come into the house at the moment. The thought spurred me to move faster and then put the mirror back in the box.

I opened the front door and slipped out, moving quietly as I didn't want to disturb the men's rest if they were still asleep. Jim Warden's hammock was empty. Peter was looking fresh and awake, swinging in his hammock with his Bible in his hands, and I tried to remember if I had ever seen him in any state besides pressed and ready. I couldn't think of a single instance.

"Good morning, Marilyn," he greeted, propping his glasses up higher on his nose and smiling at me.

"Good morning," I returned, the English words feeling strange on my tongue. "Where's Mr. Warden?"

"Using the facilities," he returned, gesturing towards the thick jungle with a shrug. "The old outhouse he built is unusable, and he hasn't finished the second one. David and I will have to finish it right away."

I sat down on Warden's hammock, being careful to balance myself in the middle. I glanced at the young man beside me, realizing that I didn't know much about him. When we were at the compound, learning Spanish or talking with the Carters, Peter had always been there; but he hadn't said much. I began to wonder simple things about him, such as his upbringing, his linguist training, his family and home state, things that I felt I should've known.

"Did you go to MLA's camp in Colorado?" I asked, feeling slightly silly.

He nodded. "Many times," he answered, closing the Bible and letting it and his hands drop onto his stomach. "I grew up on the campus. My parents were essential in starting it long before I was born and have always helped run it."

I felt even sillier, but I pushed on in my interrogation. "So you're from Colorado?"

"Yes." He left the Bible on his stomach and put his hands behind his head. Both his feet were hanging over either side of the hammock, leaving him in a comfortable position.

"So you grew up in a Christian and mission-minded family."

"Yes," he said again, and I began to realize why I didn't know much about him. For the past three months, he had been constantly at our side; yet it was nearly impossible to get him to say much. He always seemed in place when with us as a group, but when it came to one-on-one conversations, he made it hard to communicate.

Jim Warden appeared, and I quickly rose from my position on his hammock, but he waved me back. "Sit there if you like. I'm fine." He stood beside the wooden porch railing and waited, obviously expecting us to continue whatever conversation we had been having. I racked my mind, searching for something to talk about.

"When are the Miyame men returning?" Peter asked, glancing up at Warden. He was still in his lazy position, except now one of his feet was pushing the railing to make him rock back and forth.

"It could be today, tomorrow, or a week from now," he answered. "I'm confident the rubber barons will be letting them return soon."

"Why do they work for the barons?" I asked, slightly puzzled. "It pulls them away from their homes for such long periods of time, certainly they can't enjoy it."

Warden folded his arms and leaned back against the railing. "They give the Miyames radios, jewelry, clothes and other trinkets so they have to work to pay off the debt. Some of these people accept far more than they could ever pay off, according to the baron's standards. Their history is also deeply intertwined with the barons; a sinister history, full of sins on both sides."

I glanced at the native-built home peeking out from underneath the trees at the other side of the clearing, and felt a longing to reach these people, who not only sold their lives unknowingly to Colombian fortune seekers, but also gave their eternal souls to ignorance and darkness. The door suddenly opened and David shuffled out, rubbing his eyes sleepily.

"Good morning," Warden greeted, still in English.

"Good morning, Warden," David returned, closing the door behind him.

"Are the kids still asleep?" I asked.

"Yes," he answered. "Peter, how did you sleep?"

"Just fine, even with the mosquitoes," he replied, sitting up slightly. "I think I'm getting the hang of using the net properly."

David picked up the mosquito net from the ground and hung it over the railing. "Warden, didn't you say that the chief is still here?"

He dipped his head. "I believe he came back from hunting early this morning. He lives in that house over there; he wanted the runway and the foreigner's home to be built in sight of his home. You might have trouble with him. He is a stubborn man who does not want to admit that he is a guilty sinner in need of punishment."

"He might not understand it," suggested Peter.

"I have explained it to him more than any of the others. He knows how to read; the books I have translated, he has read them. He knows much more than the rest of the tribe, yet he refuses to believe it."

I hoped that Warden hadn't been forcing the Gospel down the chief's throat, because then it probably would be extremely difficult for us to convince him of the truth. I didn't want to deal with resentment. "Maybe the crop isn't ripe for harvest yet. We just need to keep planting."

Warden didn't seem too pleased with my comment, but he said nothing. David began talking over his plans for the day, and we were immediately all on board. Because a missionary had already lived here for so long, there wasn't as much to be done; the house was already built, the water tanks set up, among other things. But Warden needed to prepare us for taking over his work, we needed to make an outhouse, and we needed to settle into our home.

The day passed by quickly. We saw several Miyame women, and Peter talked to a young girl who knew Spanish. We also observed the chief walking out his house and into the jungle, but Jim Warden told us that it was not the time for talking with him.

I opened our boxes, suitcases and bags and found a place for items such as nail clippers, scissors, hair accessories and David's razor in a box beneath the desk. David used some of the wooden planks we had bought in Bogotá to create shelves on one of the walls, and I filled these with clothes. I placed our cooking utensils beside the stove on a small shelf Jim Warden had made years before.

We broke for lunch, and then the men retreated to the corner to study what Warden had learned of the Miyame language. I let the children play on the front porch, and then let myself relax a little. I wondered when I would return to the mission compound, deciding that it should be soon since the baby was almost due. I felt extremely grateful that I didn't have to give birth in the jungle; and once again I felt glad that we had airplanes, radios, hospitals and doctors.

Suddenly, Sadie, Jimmy and Dennis ran through the front door with wide eyes. "There's a bunch of people, mama," Sadie exclaimed in Spanish. "What are they doing?"

David and I made it to the porch first, followed by Warden and Peter. Men, with light-brown skin, assorted clothing and black, bright eyes, some in groups of twos and threes but most by themselves, were drifting out of the jungle and across the clearing, disappearing into the trees at the other side. Any of the ones who noticed us put on a look of indifference and kept walking. There weren't more than two dozen that we saw, but it was still a strange sight. We turned to Jim Warden, looking for an explanation.

"They've come back," he said. "There are trails through the jungle that come from where they've been working. They're coming back and going home."

David watched curiously. "You say those men were working for the rubber barons. Anthony said the rubber industry treats them unjustly – giving them cheap radios, seemingly for free, and then asking them to work off the debt. And then they make the natives work much longer than any radio should cost."

Warden's eyes darkened. "That should be the least of your worries," he said. "The rubber barons have a long, dark past. They have drowned this country's history in blood."

"What did they do?" asked Peter.

"Perhaps you will hear more of it," Warden answered, "But you won't from me. The government watches the rubber industry now, to ensure that they do not repeat their inhuman offences of the past; but what can a government do in a country like this? Insanity lies hidden in this thick jungle and cruelty runs unchecked." He shook his head. "There is not much hope for this country."

I glanced at the Miyames again and noticed that one young man held a transistor radio. He was holding this prized possession carefully and proudly, but it was enslaving him to the rubber industry, a threat unexplained and ambiguous for us. Mingled with my growing fear, I felt glad to see them; at least for a while, they could be home to tend their fields and enjoy their families.

"We shouldn't talk to them now," Warden continued. "They're tired from the long journey."

He turned and walked back inside, and we followed.

I started dinner, trying to get used to the mud stove, while David and Peter made a makeshift bed out of empty crates. They nailed some of them together and then covered it with sheets and pillows, and I hoped it would be comfortable. Right now, we had to make every scrap useful and create even bare necessities with our own hands and ingenuity. I began to feel like a real missionary.

We sat on the floor and ate, and then I settled the kids in bed. Peter, David and I stayed up late studying the results of Warden's efforts spanning several years to learn an unwritten, unknown language.

The following morning, Warden and David left to visit the chief. Before our move was complete, the chief needed to permit us to live here. Peter and I stayed at the house with the kids, working on numerous projects, waiting anxiously for them to return and hoping the introduction would go smoothly.

Finally they returned. The meeting had gone well; it didn't seem to bother the chief that Warden was leaving and a new missionary was taking his place. Peter and I were both anxious to meet Chief Jaime ourselves, and Warden assured us that it would be soon.

These first days passed by quickly. We became used to our living space, as well as the village itself. Jake's airplane came one day and carried Jim Warden away. I didn't know whether I was upset or relieved; I had felt safe with him nearby, as he knew much more than we did. But I couldn't forget the unsettling conversations we had had with him.

We had met the Miyames; now it was time to make friends with them. Years before, they had granted Jim Warden permission to settle there, and now they had approved us. They had already experienced what it was like to have a foreigner live with them. They had seen the flying airplane, the strange food, and the metal knives and nails. They didn't seem to view us as anything new. In fact, they avoided us.

At first we figured that they must be shy or wary. But after living there for a couple weeks, it seemed as if they were simply trying to ignore us and move on with their lives. We prayed and hoped that at least one Miyame would trust us and allow us to interact with them. We didn't devote much time to seeking them out; every day we seemed to find a new project we needed to do before we could fully settle down.

One day, David and Peter were sitting on the front porch taking a break. They had been hard at work clearing the jungle away from our house, but they had paused for a moment for a quick drink and a snack. As they munched on the bananas Jake had brought us on last visit, they observed a young man approaching them cautiously, but steadily.

"Hello," David called out in Spanish as the Miyame neared. He stopped, but then returned the greeting in the same language. Not many of his people knew Spanish, but there were a few, such as the chief and a few others Warden had mentioned to us. David and Peter glanced at each other hopefully.

"What are you doing?" the Miyame queried. He had stopped a yard away from the raised porch, and was looking up the stairs.

"We're eating fruit," David answered, using the general word as he didn't know the Spanish one for *banana*. "Would you like some?"

The young man seemed surprised, but he answered, "Yes, thank you." He slowly stepped on the bottom step, and then hesitated, reconsidering. Finally, he bravely walked up onto the foreigner's front porch. David and Peter were beside each other on the floor, and he seated himself across from them forming a triangle.

"What's your name?" David asked, handing him the promised banana.

"Arturo," he answered, accepting the fruit.

"I'm David, and this is Peter. How do you know Spanish?"

"I spent some time in Villavicencio, by the Meta River," he answered. "I learned Spanish, and a few English words too. There were white missionaries there who taught me many things."

Both the men looked surprised. This Miyame had seen and learned much more than the average tribesman. "Did you talk with Jim Warden much?" Peter asked.

He nodded, and his face clouded. "A little."

"Did he talk with you about Jesus?"

"Yes." He paused but then changed the subject. "I have come to ask you something." He gazed at them intently.

"What do you want to ask?" David queried.

"Do you have medicine, as the Peruvian barons do, and the Spanish in Villavicencio? Medicine for an aching head, from a rotten tooth?"

They glanced at each other, surprised. "We have medicine," David answered. "Is someone feeling unwell?"

Arturo nodded. "My mother, the chief's older sister, has a pain in her mouth and her head. I pulled her tooth for her, as a missionary did for me; but she is still in great pain. In Villavicencio, they gave me little pills. She told me to fetch the shaman, but instead I came here."

"I can give you some pills," David returned, rising to his feet and turning towards the door. "Does she live close by? Can we see her?"

"She is the chief's family; she lives in the nearest *maloka*. But the chief cannot see you; we must go around his hut carefully."

David paused. "Why?"

"He does not trust you. He does not like foreigners. I trust you because I have lived in a town and seen the pills. I know she is not hurting because of witchcraft, but because of the tooth I pulled."

"Would the chief believe us if he saw our medicine, and it worked?"

Arturo thought for a moment. "He does not like the foreigners, because they brought death to his family."

Several of the rubber barons and drug dealers in the area were from the US, and this is what Peter and David instantly thought of. "Arturo," the latter said, "You have seen many white people. Are the missionaries like the ones who bring chaos and death to your jungle, or are we different?"

"It was a missionary who brought death to the chief's family. The missionary who was here."

"Warden?" David and Peter exclaimed in unison.

Arturo nodded. "Chief Jaime asked Warden to use the radio to bring the airplane, because his son was dying. Warden would not, and the child died. Our shaman, Aniceto, said that the foreigner's airplanes bring help only to the foreigners."

He leaned forwards and spoke in a hushed voice, as if he was afraid to be overheard. "But I believe you are different. Warden did not care about us and our children, but I think you do. You gave me food and agreed to give my mother pills. You are like the missionaries I knew in Villavicencio."

"Thank you," David returned, holding out his hand. Arturo, who had learned the white man's customs, shook it firmly. "Let's get the pills, and then we'll see your mother."

The three stepped inside, where the children and I were tidying up. While David and Arturo looked through the medical bucket for the pills, Peter filled me in on who our new friend was and what they were doing. I knew I should be surprised to hear the Miyames' opinion of Jim Warden, but secretly I was pleased. It gave me more reason to dislike him. But the more I thought of it, the more wrong it seemed; would anybody, even him, deny a family access to the outside world for medical help?

6

Pilot to La Inez

After David, Peter, and Arturo left, I began making dinner. I had been in a good mood all morning, since I was looking forward to going back to the compound the next day. I was excited to stay with the Carters again, although I felt sad to leave David, Peter and the Miyames. A feeling of excitement surged through me as I thought of the baby. What color would its eyes and hair be? Which older sibling would it resemble the most?

A loud crashing sound suddenly met my ears, followed by another. It sounded like falling trees. I had heard it before, when the Miyames were building canoes together. I decided that they must be doing the same thing and I kept on cooking.

I was a little disturbed when several more crashes sounded but told myself that the Miyames might be building a new *maloka,* a large family house. I continued the preparation for the meal, assuring myself that David and Peter would see what it was on their way back.

I set the table and then decided to rest until the men returned. I felt extremely uncomfortable and dizzy as I laid on our makeshift bed.

I dozed on and off as the children played on the floor beside me, but the crashing sounds continued outside for a half hour. It had to be a really *big* maloka they were building.

A full hour later, Peter and David dashed in, their hair matted to their foreheads and their clothes dripping. They had been caught in an unexpected shower. "I didn't think it would start raining," David complained as he dried himself off. I smiled at him sleepily as I stood up and helped the children up to the table. By this time, we had built enough chairs for everyone.

"Did you give the woman the pills?" I asked after we had prayed.

David nodded, swallowing his first bite. "It took a little while for Arturo to convince her to take them, but in the end she did. After that, we talked with their family for a long time and learned a lot about their culture. By the time we left, her headache was gone. We also gave her some disinfectant and looked at her gums, I'm confident they won't get infected."

"And you didn't run into the chief?"

"No, Chief Jaime didn't see us. But now that his sister trusts us, perhaps he might." David tilted his head to the side and an expression of deep thought crossed his face. "I wonder why Warden didn't use the radio to call for help when the chief's son was sick. Jake could've brought Kara, or, they could've brought him to a hospital."

The unanswered question somehow reminded me of the falling trees. "Did you see who was cutting down trees on your way back?"

They both glanced at me, confused. "Cutting trees?" David said. "I didn't see anyone cutting trees."

"I could hear them crashing to the ground, very close to the house. It must've been at the other side of the clearing."

"We didn't notice," David answered. "Arturo's home is some little ways behind the chief's, so maybe we couldn't hear it from there. But it's too dark to see now, and I don't relish the idea of going out there with the snakes. Someone was probably building a canoe."

I didn't reply, because right at that moment my stomach seized up in a painful way. After several moments I said, “I’m not feeling well, David. I'm going to lie down.”

He nodded. “Peter will clean the dishes, and I’ll settle the kids.”

I went to bed, feeling somewhat frightened with how my stomach was acting. I woke up suddenly at around six in the morning, and realized I was having contractions. I thought of when I had given birth to Sadie, Jimmy and Dennis. The beginning had felt just like this. I grabbed David's arm and shook him violently.

“David!” I screamed. “Call Jake! Hurry! He needs to come now!”

He shot up into a sitting position and stared at me blankly for a few moments. Finally, he woke up enough to understand me and he lunged towards the transceiver radio. “La Inez to Jake Perry, are you there?”

There were a few moments of silence, but then we heard static and Kara’s sleepy voice, “Yes, we're here.”

“I’m going into labor,” I shouted before David could say anything. “Send Jake over here, please!”

“Right on it,” she answered, sounding more awake. I slumped back onto the bed and tried to calm myself down. If things went alright, I would be in Bogotá well before the baby came.

“Peter, wake up!” David called, pushing open the front door. “Help me get Marilyn and the kids ready.”

As the sleepy young man stumbled in, I wondered if he had ever imagined that his missionary life would be like this - doing dishes, dressing children and helping women in labor. I didn't think about it long, as my mind quickly returned to the severe pains tormenting my body.

“Don’t worry, Marilyn,” David said. “Jake will be here soon. We’ll get you to the compound in time.”

“The compound is a long way away from Bogotá,” Peter noted

with concern in his voice. He handed David the lantern. "She'll have to be in the pickup for an hour."

David shook his head in despair. "They can take care of her at the compound," he said. "We'll all go - Peter, you can stay here. I'll make sure she's taken care of... perhaps Jake will bring Kara. She and Joyce will be able to do something."

He talked quickly, spitting out his ideas as soon as they came to mind, and I mentally pointed out the faults in all of them. That many people couldn't even fit in Jake's airplane, for starters. Sprawled out on the bed, I wondered what Mother, Father, Steven and Meredith would think if they could see me now!

"Pilot to La Inez," the radio blared. "Do you have fuel there?"

David paused but then grabbed the radio. "Yes, we do. You left some here last time."

"Thanks. I'm running low and will need to refuel as soon as I get there."

David and Peter completed packing up the necessary baggage for a stay at the Carters'. The kids were dressed and ready, sitting sleepily in a line beside the door. Peter had just gone outside to watch for the airplane when the radio buzzed.

"Pilot to La Inez. What happened to your airstrip?"

David's eyes darkened with confusion. "I'm not sure what you mean, Jake."

The door flew open and Peter ran in, his eyes wide with horror. "David, the runway..."

"I'm circling above the strip now. Go look," Jake said.

David sprinted out the front door, followed by Peter. They scrambled down the ladder and looked towards the runway. "Oh no," David breathed.

Dozens of the trees that had once surrounded the runway had been felled and dragged onto the strip. Their gnarled branches hugged the flat surface, and some of their trunks spanned the entire width of the runway. Some of the trees were tangled together, making one think of matted hair. A couple hundred feet above, Jake's plane circled, like a bird gazing down at the chaos below.

"What happened?" Peter asked, but David didn't respond. He flew back to the house and through the door, just in time to hear Jake's voice over the radio.

"La Inez, are you there?"

David ignored him. He was digging through his tools, pulling out an axe and a saw.

"Jake, someone cut down trees and covered the runway with them," Peter explained hurriedly, eyeing his partner. "We'll get them out the way."

"We don't have time," Jake's German accent returned. "My fuel tank is dangerously low. I can't stay up here until it's cleared."

David turned and snatched the radio. "Don't you dare leave," he said through clenched teeth. "We're clearing the runway now. We'll have it done in time."

"Yes sir," Jake's doubtful voice responded. "I'll wait."

"David," I wailed pathetically, "help me!"

There was nothing more he could really do to help me, but I felt panicked and needed to say something. He glanced towards me but then scooped up Dennis, handing the tools to Peter. He called for Jimmy and Sadie, and the two of them obediently followed their father out the door. I laid on my back on the bed and kicked my feet and groaned over and over again, giving vent to the pain.

Up in the sky, Jake watched his gauge anxiously. If David and Peter didn't hurry, he wouldn't even have enough fuel to fly back to the nearest airstrip. Anthony, who could hear everything we said, called and asked how the men were progressing with the trees. Jake breathed in deeply to calm his voice before replying, "Pilot to Anthony. From here, it looks as if they're having trouble."

Peter had tied a rope to one of the trees and was pulling as hard as he could, while David hacked away caught branches and helped move it along. Many jungle trees are thin and soft, but some are monstrous with sticky sap seeping out and wood as hard as iron. Sadie and Jimmy watched wide-eyed, while Dennis clambered into the leaves and giggled.

"Peter, get the Miyames," David exclaimed, gasping for breath. "We can't do this ourselves."

The young man nodded, dropping the rope and sprinting towards Jaime's hut. Hoisting himself up the ladder onto the porch, he banged on the door, shouting in an odd mixture of Spanish, English and a few Miyame nouns he had learned. Finally, the woven door opened, and Jaime's glittering dark eyes peered out.

"The airplane needs to land," Peter said, forcing himself to speak in Spanish. "But it's covered in trees."

"I know," the young chief returned. "We did that last night. I have changed my mind about the foreigners. Warden and his airplane did nothing for us. You must pack your things and leave, and the airplane will no longer return." He shut the door.

"David, Chief Jaime did this," Peter shouted as he ran back. "We won't get any help from the Miyames."

Inside the house, Jake was speaking over the radio again. "Pilot to La Inez." I groaned and ignored it. In a more urgent voice, the German accent fired, "Pilot to La Inez." Again I did nothing. Once more, he blared, "Pilot to La Inez!"

"What?" I wailed, holding down the transmitting button.

"Marilyn, call for David. I need to talk to David!""

I staggered out of bed and opened the front door. "David!" I hollered. "Jake needs to talk to you."

Now that I could see the horrible mess on the runway myself, my heart sank lower. We were truly stranded in the jungle. The small thread that had connected us to the outside world had been snapped -

by the Miyames. I slammed the door shut and sank into a chair, laying my head on the table.

David bolted through the door and grabbed the radio. "La Inez to pilot, La Inez to pilot," he stuttered, talking too quickly for the words to make much sense.

"David, I'm sorry. I'm not even sure I have enough fuel to get to the nearest airstrip. I have to go, now."

"But Jake..."

"Keep working on the airstrip. Once I refuel, I'll come back."

"Jakob!"

"I'll come back," he repeated.

"Anthony to La Inez," we heard. "What's your situation?"

I groaned yet again. I didn't want to think about it - let alone talk about it. "We're clearing the runway," David informed him. "The Miyames won't help us. Chief Jaime did it, and I'm guessing he had several others helping him cut and drag the trees. I'm hacking them into smaller pieces, but we can't do it alone." His voice faltered, but then hardened. "We have to do it. Peter and I will have it done before Jake gets back."

"What is Marilyn's condition?"

Pathetic, I thought, but I said, "I'm fine for now."

"Joyce and I are praying for you," Anthony assured us. "God has you all safe within His hand. *Adiós.*"

David turned and ran towards the door, stopping at the shelf on his way out to look for Jim Warden's small hatchet. I clutched the pillow and repeated Anthony's words. *God has us all safe within His hand.* Somehow, that had been easier to believe yesterday. It had been easier to believe when I was sitting in the comfortable home of the Carters, with a pickup outside the door and my husband's arm around me. It had been easier to believe while we were huddled around Weldon's boxes in Olivia's living room, the children taking naps, and dinner in the oven. Now, we were completely removed from civilization, and David was hacking trees apart in a desperate effort to give his new child a safe entrance into the world.

David was halfway out the door when he halted and glanced back at me anxiously. "Do you think it's coming soon?" he asked, and I inferred he was talking about the baby.

"Not very soon," I answered, attempting to smile, but I'm glad I couldn't see my own efforts; my face probably twisted up as if I had just eaten a lemon.

"When you need help, shout out the door," he instructed me. I nodded, although I figured that by the time I desperately needed help, I wouldn't be able to shout coherently, let alone reach the door. He turned and slammed the door shut behind himself, and I was left alone.

"Why did you bring us out here, God?" I said aloud in despair. "The people don't want us here, and the chief won't let the plane in. What was the use of all that time and money spent? This mission was a complete failure!"

The world around me was silent. It seemed as if God had no answer. But then, his reply came in the soft gentle voice He uses with His children.

7

Another Delay

"*¿Hola*?" two glittering eyes peeped through the door. I hadn't even noticed it opening, but now as I looked over I realized someone was staring at me.

"Who are you?" I asked between heavy breaths. At the moment I couldn't come up with a better greeting.

A woman slipped in, her round face enveloped in a smile. Straight, jet-black hair hung over her loose dress formed from loose cloth; although my eyes were blurred, and I could neither see nor concentrate fully, the vague impression of her dress combined with her broken Spanish was enough to convince me I was speaking with one of the Miyames. She slipped into the chair next to me and laid a hand on my knee.

"Baby coming? Lucrecia help." Her Spanish words, spoken in a soft, sweet tone filled the room, permeating it with quite a different feeling than my groans had. "Lucrecia had two baby. One born in Villavicencio, where missionaries help me. I know missionary way."

The door burst open and Peter appeared. "Who are... what are..."

his voice trailed off as his eyes darted back and forth between me and Lucrecia. The Miyame woman quickly provided an explanation.

"Arturo see you cutting trees. He go to get his axe. I come and find woman having her baby."

Peter opened then shut his mouth, and his face contorted into several expressions beyond description, before he finally reckoned I was in safe hands and his expression relaxed. "This is Arturo's wife," he explained to me hastily. "We saw you come in, Lucrecia, and David sent me to see what was up. Can you help her?"

"Yes, I can," she replied.

I doubled over. "It's coming, oh, it's coming!"

Peter hurriedly blurted out what sounded like a prayer or wish for good luck of some sort and then disappeared.

The next few hours are a difficult blur in my memory, hours that I will never forget and yet never remember. I was in pain and rendered helpless in the care of an indigenous woman, who may have been helped in labor by American missionaries but most certainly had never been at the other end of the situation. But without any heed to the chaos outside, my little baby pushed herself into the world with unflagging persistence.

I do remember David coming in. His grimy, rough hand, sticky with sap and warmed by hard work, wrapped around mine and although I felt pain, I also felt peace. The next thing I was fully conscious of was him pushing a little bundle up against me. The pain had reduced considerably, and as David and Lucrecia cleaned things up I clutched the tiny life, her wrinkly, soft as velvet face up against my rubbery, sweaty one, and her teeny, squishy hand in mine.

"Pilot to La Inez," the radio crackled.

David pressed down the button. "Jake, the baby came."

"How is it? And Marilyn?"

"Both are fine for now. Marilyn is having excessive bleeding, and I'm afraid nothing here was sanitized; we need to move them to the compound whenever it's safe for the baby. I don't like either of them lying in germs and insects like this."

"Understood. How is your runway?"

"I haven't been out there for half an hour. Peter and Arturo – he's a Miyame – have been working on it."

"Let me know when it's clear. I won't leave here until it is – no need for circling in the air indefinitely." The German paused. "And you're sure Marilyn is good for now?"

"For now, yes," David assured him. "I won't leave her side, and a Miyame woman is helping us. And Peter will work as fast as possible."

A mental image flashed in my mind of the young man juggling chopping trees *and* baby-sitting all three kids, all the while communicating and thinking in several languages. I had never felt so sorry for anybody in my life.

Several minutes later the door swung open, and Jimmy and Sadie shuffled in, their little boots pattering. Peter and Arturo vaulted in next, dragging Dennis behind them. Deserting the radio, David jumped to his feet and glanced at the two men, an unasked question on his face.

An abrupt downpour commenced outside. The world outside was swelling up and bursting simultaneously, as clouds gathered and dispensed a steady deluge of water. The rain began clattering on the metal roof, dripping off the eaves and splashing onto the ground below. Peter sank into a chair, while Arturo smiled at him.

"We missed the worst of the rain," the Miyame observed.

"The strip's clear, David," Peter said, removing his glasses and wiping the water off with his sleeve. "Several of Arturo's friends came and helped us."

David fell back into his chair and grabbed the radio. "La Inez to pilot - runway's ready, Jake."

"Really?" the German's voice sounded incredulous. "Kara and I are on our way."

David rotated in his chair to face Arturo. "Thank you," he said softly. "You and Lucrecia... I don't know what we would've done if you hadn't come to help."

"We trust you," Arturo said, "And you helped my mother. She and her husband and more family were willing to come because of your pills and your kind words."

"Many hands made light work," Peter commented, pushing his round glasses back up his nose. He still looked the perfect picture of composure to me, although his soiled clothes and dirty, bleeding hands were signs of his recent exertions. "Heavens, is that the baby?"

"Yes, and we're most likely disturbing her and Marilyn's rest," said David, snapping back to the current situation. The rain outside pounded louder. "Peter, we can't send the kids outside. Let's settle them for a rest in the corner and make everything quiet."

As soon as the word *quiet* left his mouth, a ferocious pounding began on the door. Peter opened it, and a young man stepped in, chattering in the Miyames' strange gurgle. His voice was bounding first high then low, and he was obviously very agitated. I laid my cheek against my sleeping baby's and tried to block the stream of obtrusive noise from her ears.

"Arturo, who is he and what does he want?" David asked despairingly.

"This is Misael, the chief's son," Arturo explained. "He says his father is dying and demands to see the missionaries."

With mouth agape Peter glanced at David, who in turn looked towards me. "Well, go see him!" I exclaimed with a wave of my hand. "And bring the medical box."

"I should stay with you," David said hesitantly. "Someone needs to take care of the children."

"I've never talked with the chief," Peter objected. "He recognizes you as the head missionary, you should come with me."

"He's right, David. Perhaps Lucrecia can help with the children."

David ran his fingers through his hair. "I'll go. I know Lucrecia has good intentions, but I'm not comfortable leaving you with her. Peter, could you watch the little ones?"

Peter hid his disappointment with a little smile and a shrug. "Of course, David."

After pulling on his poncho and boots and tucking the medical box underneath his arm, David quickly departed with Arturo and the chief's son.

Sadie and Jimmy, being nearly six and four, understood the need for quiet when Peter explained it to them, and they both settled in their hammocks with books. The books were ones that the Carters had given to us, and were made up of mostly pictures, with a few words in Spanish on each page. Dennis was two years old and not at all interested in being quiet. He was tired, and tiredness in toddlers almost always evokes screaming or yelling of some sort. I was on my side facing my baby, but in the small room I could clearly hear Peter's efforts behind my back to interest Dennis in toy soldiers (which were actually clothespins). Being a mother, I could easily picture the scene.

Peter finally resorted to rocking Dennis to sleep. He sat down in a hammock with one foot hanging over the side resting on the chair, pushing gently. Cuddling Dennis in his lap, he read one of the children's books, which calmed my son down somewhat. As the steady, methodical swaying began to take its magical effect, Peter started singing a hymn softly. The words were familiar ones, etched into my mind since childhood. "Rock of Ages, cleft for me – let me hide myself in thee!"

I turned slowly and painfully onto my back, trying to straighten the ruffles and folds of the mix-matched sheets I was lying in. I could just barely see the top of Peter's head swinging back and forth, slowly, to the beat of his song. The rhythm of his swinging had a soothing effect; with each swing I felt a smudge more of tension wiped off my sweaty forehead. The lyrics, sung so softly, were subtly powerful; the room had been transformed into a quiet, tranquil haven.

Before I turned my face towards my baby, something caught my eye. Just above Peter's head I could see the shelf David had built. The men had ruffled through it hurriedly that morning; clothes were unfolded and jumbled, dirty and clean alike piled on top of each other, with the children's ponchos thrown on top. Amid the mess lay a reassuring token of peace that I hadn't noticed before; David must've brought it from America in his personal bag and laid it there in the past couple days. It was a bundle of light blue cloth, which I knew wrapped an old timeworn book.

I decided to wait until Dennis was asleep and then ask Peter to hand the book to me. Seconds after making this decision, I changed my mind. That copy was too fragile for me to read at the current moment, as shaky and weak as I was. I tried to remember where I had left my own Bible. My thoughts turned into a different channel as I gradually became aware of a buzzing noise, growing louder and louder. Lucrecia smiled at me, gurgled something in Miyame, and then slipped outside.

A strange feeling came over me. The tie to humanity was mended. With Jake's arrival we were reconnected with civilization once again; within minutes I would be transported through the air and brought to a house with electricity. But the feeling wasn't one of peace, or even excitement; it was of wonder.

It's easy to say God is with you, but harder to believe it, and sometimes it is nearly impossible to really, really believe it. Had I been relying on technology to save me? God was my protection and my rock, not man and his inventions. When airplanes and radios and hospitals failed me, God was still there. I marveled at this simple fact that I had believed so long, for now it had begun to move from my brain to my heart.

I propped myself up as far as I dared. The bed was growing uncomfortable; I was convinced that one of the crates had shifted and I was sinking into a miniature ditch. The sheets were the most rebellious things I had dealt with in a long time; I couldn't find corners, only random, folded edges and twisted, intertwined lumps and knots. For a lover of order, it was maddening. However, after a brief attempt to fix it I tried to ignore it, knowing that I couldn't straighten it out successfully unless both me and baby got out.

The door swung open and sweet Kara bustled in. "You look a mess," she declared, immediately beginning to tidy up the floor. I realized that the mess extended beyond me and my bed – the children's boots lay on the floor, the clothes that weren't cluttering the shelf were scattered about in random places, and part of this morning's uneaten breakfast that I had prepared last night sat on the mud stove. Energetic Kara set things right in a matter of minutes.

She then helped me straighten up, and she even put my hair in a neat braid. I had never before noticed how big a difference combing one's hair could make on the nerves. Baby woke up, and Kara moved both me and her aside so she could fix up the bed. She gave me a cup of water and as I lay back down, I felt refreshed beyond expression.

"Have the children eaten?" she asked.

I racked my mind, attempting to remember the sequence of events. The frantic proceedings of that morning hadn't left any room for us to complete even the simplest household tasks. "No, I guess not," I admitted, feeling like a broken record, as all moms do at some time. Peter and Dennis were both fast asleep in the hammock, the former's foot still hanging out; Sadie and Jimmy were huddled on the floor in the corner, exhausted and, I realized, hungry.

Jake pushed open the door. His tall frame more than filled the doorway; as he stepped in his yellow hair scraped against the top. "Hallo, Marilyn. How are you feeling?"

"Fine for now, thank you," I said.

The German glanced towards Peter, who was still snoozing. "Where's David?" he asked.

"He went to visit the chief, who is reportedly dying." For some reason, I didn't feel as concerned about the chief as I probably should've. I was about to be whisked away from La Inez anyway, and by the time I came back from Bogotá this whole ordeal would be over, whether the chief lived or died. I wasn't even interested in hearing what his problem was. I just wanted to take care of my precious baby.

"Does he need medical attention?" Kara asked anxiously. Her heart was always big enough to hold everybody.

"I don't know any details," I confessed, "Except that he is dying and wanted to see a missionary."

"That could be good or bad for you," Jake said thoughtfully. "If the chief is asking for help, and David is able to help him, that's an open door. But this chief may've asked for David so he could fume and curse him before he dies." He pulled a chair closer to the bed and sat down. "Do you know what his plan was? Should I be loading you and the kids up into the Cruiser now, or should I wait until he gets back?"

"Wait for him to come back," said I. "He shouldn't be gone long, and he most likely heard you fly in."

And so we waited. Kara fixed some food for Sadie and Jimmy, and although we tried to let them sleep Peter and Dennis both woke up. Only a few minutes passed by before the door opened and David slipped in, water trickling down his poncho and spattering into puddles across the floor as he walked towards me.

"Marilyn, could you wait a couple of hours?" he asked his question lightly, but I could feel the pleading undertone. "I would stay with you. It's just a small delay. You'll be at the compound by evening."

My heart was sinking, but I tried to put a bold face on it. "I certainly don't prefer it, but it wouldn't kill me..."

"Why can't I take her now?" Jake spoke up.

"Because I want you to fly Chief Jaime to Bogotá first," David said firmly. He never apologized in situations like this, when he changed plans and priorities to help others; I usually loved him for it, but today was a different matter. Chief Jaime had done this to us. It was his fault I wasn't sleeping peacefully in the compound or Bogotá right now on fresh sheets and a bed that stayed in one piece. I felt he had picked a wonderful time to have a sudden attack of whatever was ailing him, so we could leave him in his dirty hut to see what it felt like to live without an airplane.

But David's sweet-tempered voice slowly levelled my mental hills of anger. "The chief will have to lie across the backseat, with somebody with him to take care of him. We can't fit Marilyn into the front with the baby, at least not comfortably. If Marilyn waits, it means sacrificing a clean bed. If the chief waits, it may mean his life."

I rubbed my face with my hands, and then sighed. "Take him," I said, "Just take him, quick."

David gave a nod and glanced towards the German pilot. "Jake, help me carry him. Kara, perhaps you can ride with them and keep an eye on him – I think he has some sort of intestinal bleeding, or something similar. He's very dizzy and was throwing up."

The two men strode out the door, Kara pausing a moment to hand Dennis a banana and then following. "Do you need my help?" Peter asked sleepily, straightening his glasses.

"No, stay with Marilyn," David said, and the door shut. I leaned against the pillows and sighed, gently stroking the baby's hair. It felt like soft feather-down. I watched an impressively large beetle struggling up the sheet draped over us. It kept slipping, and it seemed to have little sense of direction; but slowly, it made its way higher and closer to my leg. With it openly exposed on the sheet, I knew Dennis would spot it soon and play with it like a toy.

Out of nowhere, I began humming a tune, stroking the baby's head in rhythm.

'Rock of ages, cleft for me; let me hide myself in thee...'

8

Colombian Autumn

"Have you heard what was wrong with the chief?" I asked sleepily, scooting into a sitting position and yawning. The sun was streaming through the tiny window of the small, neat room I was in, at the mission compound outside Bogotá. Just a few minutes after I had woken up, when I was contemplating the sweet difference between this bed and the one in La Inez, Joyce Carter had come in with a glass of juice.

"Ruptured appendix," she said, in answer to my question. "He is a living miracle. If Jake Perry had not already been in La Inez, there might not have been enough time to get him to the hospital. A visiting surgeon from Santa Marta was there giving a lecture, who had enough skill to fix the damage without complications. He even did it for free, as a demonstration in his lecture." The wrinkles beneath her eyes crinkled into a smile. "God is good!"

I smiled back, savoring the refreshing fruit juice. "Where's David?" I asked.

"He is outside with the little ones. They have eaten already," she informed me. "He told me tomorrow is Sadie's birthday, so I am planning to make a special treat. Do you know what she would like?"

Sadie's sixth birthday... I had almost forgotten. Hopefully David would grab her some special trinket from the Bogotá market. "Honestly, she thinks a fruit salad is exciting," I said. "In Washington, for her first few birthdays, I made cupcakes." I smiled at the memory, and then hoped she wouldn't remember. Fruit salad would have to do.

"Oh, I can make cupcakes," Joyce exclaimed. "I've made them many times before. I just have to ask Anthony to buy me some things for the frosting."

"You don't have to," I remonstrated, "Sadie is fine with anything."

Joyce strode out of the room with a decided air. "Cupcakes it is!"

When lunchtime rolled around, David brought the kids into my room. They brought their meal with them, but were far too excited over the baby to eat it. We gave Sadie, Jimmy, and Dennis supervised turns holding baby Mary. Ever since she was born we hadn't had a chance to enjoy her as a family; now, in the peaceful atmosphere of the mission compound, we found the perfect opportunity. Little Mary reminded me most of Sadie in looks, with brown hair just a little lighter than the boys'. In temperament she already was proving to be most like Jimmy, who had been my calmest baby.

We finally steered the children towards their food, and they all settled on the floor with their plates. David sat on the edge of the bed, holding Mary. "I bet the chief will let us back after this," he said confidently. "Now he knows we're different."

Different than what? Jim Warden? I let my mind slip into unpleasant thoughts. Jim Warden had managed to make the chief hate him; he was nastier than I had originally thought. Now, I comforted myself, I could rest without a doubt that his charges against Weldon Cole were fabricated lies.

Sadie woke us all up the next morning, reminding us of her special day. Joyce made her signature scrambled eggs for breakfast, omitting the peppers at Sadie's request. I felt a little embarrassed that my six-year-old refused to eat peppers, but Joyce simply smiled and altered her recipe.

Shortly after the meal, Jake flew in with Peter. I was in bed most of that day, but David kept me informed. "Jake and Peter are going to visit the chief in the hospital," he told me. "It'll be a while before he can go home, I'm afraid, but I'm glad he's healing."

"Mama, the cupcakes!" Sadie shouted, rushing into the room. "There are cupcakes, Mama, six of them!" she held up her little fingers, counting out six. "This many. They even have frosting!"

"I think we've won our first victory with the Miyames," David continued. "All the pieces are falling together. It was nothing short of a miracle."

Shortly after, we heard an update on the chief. He was recovering slowly, and after a few days in bed was enjoying being wheeled around in a chair exploring the hospital. Jake and David went to visit him, and came back with good news: the chief was willing to give us another chance. *Thank you, God,* I remember praying, *We'll do something big in this tribe for You, just wait and see!*

Whatever *big* thing we were going to do, it didn't happen right away. David and I lingered at the compound. We both felt that our newborn was safer here, where germs and viruses were less prevalent. It was better to be safe than sorry, we decided. Mary would handle the jungle better if she was a few weeks old opposed to days.

We didn't waste our time; there was always plenty of room to increase our Spanish, which our friend Alejandro was more than happy to help us with. Anthony would quiz David on Spanish as they did repair jobs around the compound, and Joyce even spoke it with the children as they helped her with chores around the house. While life hummed along, I spent most of my time with my baby, holding her close and watching her grow.

It was a refreshing few weeks of our lives; we had the chance to wind down after the excitement in La Inez. All the stress we had piled up in our short time there slowly dissolved into the sea of happiness we found ourselves in. Peter spent some of the time with us, and we worked on the Miyame vocabulary charts Jim Warden had given us and went over the portion of the New Testament he had written.

The time of year rolled in that we would normally call Fall or Autumn. Here we called it wet and wetter – as we did every season from thereafter. Back at home, it had always been my favorite season. My family had always celebrated every moment of Autumn, and I had carried that tradition into my own. The smell of cinnamon, coming out of the chilly outdoors into a cozy room, a crackling fire in the hearth, wearing snug jackets, making pies and mashed potatoes with gravy, sending a rush of warm hot chocolate into a chilled body – this year these things turned into memory rather than reality. But as long as we were together, I figured, our family could do without.

On a warm and rainy day, Jake flew us back to La Inez. I was glad to see how comfortable he was flying even in the rain: rarely was there worse weather, which meant that just about nothing could stop him flying in if we needed it. In our long absence from the jungle, we had already almost forgotten the excitement of Mary's birth. As the Piper Cruiser rolled down the narrow strip with the tribesman's hut and the white man's house in clear sight, it felt like we were arriving for the first time all over again.

I had almost the same disappointment this time around as I settled on our packing boxes and pillows that night. We had been advised against a bed like this since the beginning, because of the easy access for bugs; we were always told that hammocks were the wisest choice. David and I had chosen to try an actual bed that touched the ground, though, and we had never minded the inconveniences too much. But tonight nothing was comfortable. After tossing from side to side, which seemingly bruised my hips and shoulders with every turn, I began eyeing Dennis's hammock. It was empty, as he had climbed in bed with us.

After spending only a few minutes in the hammock I was disgusted with it. Though I had slept in hammocks back in Colorado for training, I had been one of the few people who never found them comfortable. At last I collapsed back on our packing-crate bed and after resigning myself to misery, I fell asleep.

The next morning, though, we all felt brighter. Lucrecia and Arturo came by early in the morning. As I folded clothes, brushed hair and killed spiders, I talked with Lucrecia about her understanding of salvation. It was limited, so I patiently went over God's good news and answered her many questions.

Arturo, meanwhile, helped David and Peter work on projects around the house. Our family was settling in nicely, so now it was time to focus on our original mission – evangelism and translation.

We told Arturo and Lucrecia to invite their friends and family to a daily Bible study each evening. "I am not sure any will come," Arturo told us, a cloud passing over his brow. A bright smile replaced his doubt as he assured us, "But we will come."

The two of them and one of their young sons were the first attendants of our Bible study. David read a chapter or two from his Spanish gospel, explained it and expounded a few points, and then we worked on translating a verse with their help and input.

Jake Perry flew in once with a treat from the Carters. There was a wire cage in his backseat, with five airsick chickens inside. David and I were thrilled, while our children were beyond excited. "I'm going to name this one," Sadie announced, pointing through the wire. David was carrying the cage off the airstrip, and the children were clustered around him.

"No, that one's mine," Jimmy objected. "Can't I name that one, Daddy? And this one?"

David set the cage down and began prying it open with his pocketknife. "Don't let them out," exclaimed Sadie in alarm, "They'll fly away and get lost!"

"They'll be fine," David assured her. "They're very tired; I'm just going to let them stretch a little. Do you want to help me build a little pen for them?"

"Yes, and I've already got names for all of them!" she said, helping him pull it open.

"I wanted to name one," Jimmy complained.

David carefully lifted one out. "This one is Sadie's," he said, "Because it's the first one to walk around our home." The chicken cautiously pecked at the ground, tilted its head, and then waddled a few paces away.

"I want to name it Firstborn," Sadie said solemnly, "After me."

David glanced at me incredulously, and I gave a lopsided smile and shrugged.

"This one," he continued, "Is Jimmy's."

"His name is Billy," Jimmy said.

"A respectable name for a chicken," David said, giving him a poke. "This one is Dennis's."

Dennis gazed at it with his big blue eyes. "Chicken," he said.

"Another respectable name," David said. "Mary gets to name this one."

Sadie helped him lift it out. "Mary can't talk, so can I name it?"

"No, this one is Mary's. We'll call it Mary's Chicken until she can talk, that way she can name it all by herself."

"And what about the last one?" Jimmy asked. Gingerly he helped David set it out. "Does Mamma get to name this one?"

"Its name is Sammy," I said. "I wonder if we gave these chickens appropriate names, being that they're girls?"

Firstborn, Billy, Chicken, Mary's Chicken, and Sammy adapted quite well to the jungle, and the kids enthusiastically helped David build them a pen and a solid coop. I could only laugh. Growing up, we had always had at least thirty chickens and I never cared any more for them than I did for all the other animals around our place. But chickens were something special out here.

December rolled in, but before the Christmas season could begin David and I celebrated our eighth anniversary. David had promised me a break from housework, and I had promised him my full attention; naturally, this meant we were planning on leaving Peter at home babysitting while we went on a walk into the jungle. I hadn't explored much, as I was too nervous to do it alone. David and Peter had been led on a few tours by Arturo, and were beginning to learn their way around.

I woke up early that morning and slid quietly out of bed, careful not to wake David or the baby. I had tried making makeshift hair curlers out of wads of cloth, and now I carefully pulled them out, sitting in front of the mirror. To my amazement, my hair had curled. I ran my fingers along my scalp, straightening out my part, and then I slid a hair clip up the roots of one of my large curls. I grinned, and my reflection grinned back. I knew my curls would fall out in a few hours, but for now I was gorgeous.

With the trek through the jungle in mind, I pulled on some denim jeans, and a white cotton shirt with flowers around the neckline. Tugging my rubber boots snugly over my feet, I stepped outside onto the porch. Peter was awake and dressed, lying in his hammock with his Bible, like he was every morning. He always woke up first, then me, then David, and then the kids.

"Good morning, Peter," I greeted, grabbing his hammock and giving it a swing.

"Good morning, Marilyn." He slid his legs over the side, carefully balancing himself against the swaying. "Yours and David's eighth anniversary, right?"

"Yes," I answered. I leaned against the porch railing, which creaked and bowed a little. "It's today. Remember we're planning on a walk this afternoon; are you sure you'll be all right with the kids?"

He waved my concern away. "I'll be fine. I'll just stay on the front porch here holding Mary, and let the kids play out here."

"If Mary gets fussy, find Arturo or Lucrecia and send them to fetch us," said I, anxiously. He just smiled and kept swinging.

I yawned, sniffed the morning air, and cracked my knuckles. The air felt warm, and there was definitely less moisture in it that gave me hope of an outing without rain. I glanced at Peter, who was rocking back and forth, back and forth. I remembered the first morning we had spent on this porch, and the questions I had asked about his past; I had never learned anything after that.

"Your parents are some of the founders of that linguist camp in Colorado, aren't they? How long have they been married?" I asked. Anniversaries were already a topic, so I thought I'd start the conversation from there.

He snapped his Bible shut. "They're not together anymore," he said. "They divorced when I was fifteen."

"Oh." I had never met any of the top people at the linguist camp, but I had always imagined Peter's family as a happy unit running it. I shrugged. "That's too bad, I'm sorry."

The door swung open, and bleary-eyed David gazed out. "Marilyn, the baby has been crying and crying," he said.

"I'm sorry, I didn't notice."

"How could you not hear her?" David thumped the wall. "It's see-through, I can't imagine it being sound-proof."

"That reminds me, where's that new house you promised me?" I said drily, following him inside, where the baby was howling that persistent, repetitive scream peculiar to babies her age. "I was in a conversation, it's not my fault I didn't hear her."

"I'm not blaming you for anything, I was just asking you to get her."

"You could've found a nicer way than *she's crying and crying why aren't you coming!*" I mimicked his irritated voice with a good deal of exaggeration.

He shrugged on his shirt and grabbed a banana. "I did not say it like that."

I gave an exasperated sigh. "Yes, you did."

He swung open the door. "I'll be outside if you need me."

"Not with that attitude."

The door shut.

I quieted the baby and then fed the children as they woke up. I tidied up the house, and then stepped outside to the clothesline where I had left clothes to dry the day before. As I filled my arms with laundry, I glanced around for David and Peter. I couldn't see them; they had probably gone and found something useful to do.

Lunch time rolled around and I still couldn't see them. I fixed the children food again and then sat on Peter's hammock with sleeping Mary nestled in my lap. I had planned to try making *casabe* bread that day, but instead I sat and worried. David never disappeared for this long without telling me beforehand. The absence of both frightened me even more; something must've happened.

At last I slipped out of the hammock and went into the house. I laid Mary on the bed gently, instructed Sadie to keep her brothers in the house and quiet, and then I went outside. I crossed the runway and walked past the chief's house; a couple minutes of jogging and I had reached the first *maloka.*

Each *maloka* housed a family: grandparents, parents, sons, daughters, in-laws, children, aunts, uncles and anyone else deemed fit to group into that particular family. The chief had the smallest, and whatever family he had that couldn't fit inside lived in this *maloka.* Hearing voices, I ran around it, instantly spotting Lucrecia. She and several others were weaving long, tough leaves into baskets.

I called her name, but she didn't notice. I jumped over a few rotting branches and scrambled up the slope to the level they were on. "Lucrecia," I repeated, coming up behind her. I was intending to ask her to either watch my kids or search for the men; preferably the latter, as I would get lost in a matter of minutes. But as she turned towards me, a sinking feeling entered my stomach. Her face was white, her cheeks stained with tears and her eyes glossy.

"Lucrecia, what's wrong?" I asked, stumbling over my Spanish in my concern. "What is wrong?" I repeated, clearer this time. She only shook her head sadly and turned back to her work. I turned and skidded down the slope, ran past the *maloka* and through the trees and foliage, sprinted across the runway and towards our house. Something must be wrong with our only two friends, and she wouldn't talk about it.

I thumped up our porch and went inside. Mary was crying and Dennis was bawling; Sadie had spilled my large jar of rice all over the floor, and was trying to scoop it up with her grubby hands. Jimmy flung his arms around my middle and squeezed.

"What's wrong with Dennis?" I asked wearily, sitting on the edge of my bed and smoothing Mary's hair.

Sadie was shoving mounds of rice together to form a rice mountain. "He was hitting Jimmy, so I smacked him."

"Don't smack your brother, just tell Mama next time." I picked up Dennis and soothed him, mixing in with my comforting strain a few reprimands for hitting Jimmy. Mary quieted after I fed her a few bites of cooked vegetables left on the counter. By the time the rice mess was cleaned up and the house was in order, I had almost forgotten about Lucrecia.

The door swung open and Peter and David came in. I glanced up with a look of wearied annoyance, letting my displeasure at their absence show. David slumped on the bed, kicking off his boots and shooting back a look of exasperation. Peter sank onto the chair by the desk.

"So," I began, after a moment of silence, "Where were you?"

"Most of the men are going back to the rubber barons," David said. "Pete and I ran across them in the jungle, and we've spent hours trying to convince them to not go, or pay off their debt and accept nothing more. But every one of them has a debt to repay, and every one of them feels the need to break their backs for these crooked men in exchange for a few trinkets and cheap electronics. None of them would tell us about the barons' dark history Warden alluded to, either."

I sighed. Neither of us were having a very good day. As I was ruminating over every moment that had gone wrong, David jumped to his feet and began pulling his boots back on.

I watched him for a moment. "Where are you going?" I asked in mild surprise.

"I promised to go on a walk with you," he answered. "And I don't break my promises, do I?"

He held out his hand, and a laugh tumbled out of my dry throat. "No, you don't." I took his hand and he pulled me to my feet and towards the door. As I shouted directions to Peter and admonished my children to be good, he towed me out the door. As it shut behind us, he put his arm around me and we walked into the jungle.

9

Tapirs and Rubber

I scrambled down the steep slope, grabbing bushes below and branches above to keep me from sliding. I had been to the river many times, down the well-worn trail behind our house, but David was taking me to a bank farther up that required a lot more effort. It was getting late, and as much as I loved the alive feeling of the jungle, I was worried about Peter and the kids and I was ready to head back. Dusk lasted only a few minutes and came at six every day, and I didn't want to get caught in the dark. I dodged around some vines and sprinted over a few feet to catch up with David.

"*¿Hola?*" Two eyes peered at us from around a tree. My heart jumped into my throat and I gripped David's arm. Arturo stepped out, and my heart slid back into place.

"Hello, Arturo," David replied in Spanish. "What's up?"

The Miyame fidgeted, holding his hands behind his back and scraping a line in the ground with his bare foot. "I have come."

"For what?"

He looked up at us with his dark eyes. "To say farewell."

My eyebrows tilted upwards. "Where are you going?"

"To the rubber forest. I will be working there."

I glanced at David, my mouth dropping open. He shook his head and quickly objected. "Arturo, you can't do that. The rubber barons are cruel and they don't care about their workers. They don't pay you fairly."

He shrugged, stretching out his palms. "I am in debt to them, and I promised to come again. You want me happy, but I do not mind the rubber men. They give me work. Is that not what matters?"

"Arturo," I said pleadingly.

"Goodbye," he said, using the first English word we'd heard him say. He repeated the farewell in his own language, and then he was gone.

We stood silent for several moments, stunned and crushed. The only Miyame who didn't ignore us, our only Bible study attendant, our only chance of a convert... he had deserted us for the rubber barons with the rest of his imprudent tribe. David stuffed his hands into his pockets and began walking, his shoulders hunched and his head hanging. I followed. The air hung heavy and hot. As the river came into view, I reached out and touched David's arm.

"David," I said softly.

He looked at me, his eyes red and his face flushed. "How are we going to do anything without him?" he asked in a low, quivering voice, "And how could I let my friend walk blindly into this trap?"

I was without an answer. I wrapped my arms around him as my only reply. After a few moments he returned the embrace. "Lord," he said at length, "help us not to be discouraged. Be with Arturo, and let all the men come home safely. And let us make a difference, if even a small one."

"Amen," I murmured.

Abandoning our quest for the river, we walked back up to the house. As it came into sight I quickened my pace, nearly running up the steps and through the door. It was becoming dark rapidly. Dennis and Jimmy were asleep in their hammocks, while Sadie lay awake in hers. Peter was walking around in circles holding my baby, who was crying softly, in that exhausted, half-hearted way that meant she was far beyond tired.

"Thank you, Peter," I said, taking Mary. "How did you get the boys to sleep?"

"Marilyn, did you not hear that?" David stepped partway inside, glancing over his shoulder. "As we were coming up, that noise outside?"

"Noise?" I said distractedly, cradling Mary and rummaging through my bedsheets. "Peter, do you know where her blanket is?"

He picked it up off the shelf and handed it to me. "Dennis and Jimmy weren't minding very well," he told me, "So I told them to lie in their hammocks until they were ready to be good. As you can see, they were bent on being stubborn."

I laughed. "I'm sorry we were gone for so long. These four are a handful sometimes."

"So you didn't hear it?" David was still in the doorway.

"I hope you enjoyed your walk. I know this anniversary hasn't gone exactly as planned," Peter said.

"Oh, it's gotten worse. We met Arturo in the jungle." I sat down on the bed.

David walked outside, pulling the door behind him. "I'm going to see what that noise was."

"All right, David," I called after him. I wasn't even sure of what he was talking about, and I'd forgotten that I had the flashlight. Mary was already closing her eyes, and yawning as I wrapped her in her blanket. "Arturo has left for another rubber harvest, Peter."

"Arturo?" He straightened his glasses. "Marilyn, why? I thought he would know better than this, I thought he understood."

I nodded. "I know." I rocked Mary back and forth, and her eyelids drooped. "I saw Lucrecia earlier, she was just about in tears. Arturo didn't give us much of a chance to talk with him, he merely said goodbye and left."

Peter glanced at the door. "Does David have a flashlight? I'll bring him mine."

He swung open the door and I turned my full attention to Mary. She had fallen asleep already, her soft cheek resting against my arm. I leaned back against the pillows and smiled, running my fingers through her curly hair. She had grown quite a headful in her nearly six months of life. There were still good things in this world, I decided.

"David!"

I heard Peter shout my husband's name in alarm. There was a muffled cry from outside. My blood turned to water and then I panicked. I dropped Mary onto the bed and ran out the door, ignoring her cries. The world outside was in deep shadow. I staggered through the heavy air, fumbling to turn my flashlight on. I could hear a strange grunting noise, and crashing, shaking noises, and David calling for help, mingled with exclamations of pain. Peter was shouting, too; I couldn't tell what either of the men were saying. I tripped over a root and fell over, but I was on my feet again in a second.

In the light of my flashlight, I saw a large creature race into the trees, with the speed of a pony and the sloppy trot of a pig. Ignoring it, I fumbled through the dark toward where I had heard the men's voices. "David?" I called. "David, where are you?"

"Right here," Peter called softly. "Marilyn, do you have a light?"

"Yes," I answered. The night was strangely quiet now. I strained my ears for any sound from David, but I heard nothing. "Where are you? What happened? What was that?"

"I suppose it was a tapir," replied Peter's voice. "It was big, whatever it was."

"Oh." I took a step into the inky blackness in the direction of his voice, and pushed a vine out of my face. I shone the light right into Peter's face. "There you are!"

David was prostrate on the ground, face down. Peter was kneeling beside him, his hand on my husband's head. Before I could say anything, I heard Sadie's voice say "Mama?"

I glanced over my shoulder and saw her, standing outside without a flashlight or shoes.

"Sadie!" I exclaimed. "Come here, now, like a good girl. Follow my light."

She walked towards me, placing each little bare foot ahead of the other. I shuddered as I saw a small snake slither away just a couple feet from her toes. She caught up with me and as I laid my hand on her shoulder I could feel her trembling. I pressed her head against my side. "Don't worry, Mama's got you. Watch your feet for snakes. Come on."

I took her hand and step by step, we made our way to the men. Now I could hear David's heavy breathing, and a slight groan. I shone the flashlight on him and instantly Sadie's grip on my hand tightened. His right sleeve was torn and matted to his skin with blood. What concerned me more was the traces of red showing in his dark hair. I dropped to my knees and handed the flashlight to Peter.

"David?" I touched his shoulder above his wounded arm. "David, can you hear me?"

"Yes, I'm fine." He touched my hand with his. "Just... dizzy. Is it gone?"

"Is what gone?" Sadie glanced around.

David lifted his head a few inches and glanced at our daughter. "Sadie!" he managed a weak smile. "Hello, girl. Daddy's got a bit of a scrape," he grimaced at his arm, "but he'll be alright."

More than a bit, I thought. "What happened?"

"It must have been one of those tapirs we're always told about. It surprised me and I surprised it. I'm not quite sure of what happened after that... it knocked me over, and I think it bit me. When I got up again I tried running, but I kept crashing into trees and falling over things and it caught up with me a couple times. Then Peter came and scared it away."

"Are you in a lot of pain?" I asked. He winced as Peter and I helped him sit up.

"Just a little banged up." He brushed some dirt off his canvas pants. His knuckles were scraped and bleeding. "This arm hurts, though, quite a bit. This kind of thing only happens to us ignorant *gringos*, I'm guessing. Pete, could you help me up?"

Peter stood and helped hoist David to his feet. I rose also, taking hold of Sadie's hand. Slowly our procession trudged through the jungle trees back toward the clearing. The men staggered in the lead, David leaning heavily on Peter, and Sadie and I brought up the rear, with the flashlights to brighten up the way.

We all clambered up the porch steps and then David collapsed. I put Sadie into her hammock and then joined Peter. He was cleaning up the tapir bite, and then I helped him put on a temporary bandage. My shaking fingers went over the work somewhat sloppily, but Peter tightened it up and soon the arm was wrapped nicely. David was still off-balance, in a light-headed form of shock. We made him stay quiet as we cleaned him up.

"Thank you, Peter," I said as we finally sat back. "You wrapped that up better than I could've alone."

"I've done it many times before, though never for real," said Peter. "At the camp in Colorado, my mom does the foreign missions first aid class every year. I used to help her demonstrate how to wrap up animal bites among other things."

I nodded, and then rubbed my eyes and fought against a yawn. It felt strange to think of crawling into bed and sleeping after the fright and excitement, but I was tired. "Should we call Kara now?" I asked sleepily, reaching up and braiding my hair. "And ask her to fly over with Jake?" A yawn tried to surface, but I pushed it down.

"They can't come over till morning, so we might as well wait till then," Peter said. "Kara will know if David needs stitches or not. I'm pretty sure there's no bone broken, but she'll know best."

I lost my fight against the yawn. Peter yawned, too. Laughing sleepily we wished each other goodnight and he went off to his hammock, while I snuggled down with Mary. After another yawn, I closed my eyes and went to sleep.

The next morning dawned warm and dry. After giving Kara a quick call I chatted with Anthony and Joyce, telling them all about our anniversary, Arturo, the rubber barons, the tapir and David's arm. When I finally forced myself to put down the radio, I plunged into the same old everyday grind – fixing breakfast, dressing the kids, cleaning the house.

"The airplane, Mama!" Sadie shouted at about a quarter to twelve. I was behind the house by the tank of water that filled up our bucket sink, picking up the dishes I had washed earlier. I ran around to the front porch and went inside.

"Jake's here," I said, sliding the dishes onto the shelf. David was on the bed, slowly pulling his boots on. He had spent the morning resting at my request. "Kara will be in here in a moment, you don't need to get up."

"I'm fine," he insisted. "I'm just a little sore." He lifted himself up and staggered toward the door, his good arm pressing against the wall to support himself. "I think I pulled a muscle," he grumbled under his breath.

I put the last dish in place and then opened the door for him. We stepped out onto the porch just as Kara came walking up. I could see Jake on the runway, fussing over his airplane. The kids had run over to him and were eagerly watching him refuel.

"Had a bit of a scare last night, didn't you?" Kara said, walking up the steps. She gave me a hug and a pat on the back. "I bet there's no damage to be concerned about. There's not much a tapir can do to you besides make you uncomfortable."

I glanced at David, and from the look on his face he was the very definition of uncomfortable.

"Let's go inside so David can sit," Kara said, hustling us through the door.

"Tapirs don't normally do that, do they?" David asked, lowering himself into a chair. "Every photo I've seen of them, it just seems like a pig-like creature with some, oh, I don't know, elephant-like traits, nosing around. I would've thought they'd be skittish things."

"They are," said Kara. "But like every wild animal, they're a little unpredictable. But they are normally very shy of humans."

"*Gringo*," he muttered.

"You should've had a flashlight," she continued. "It's basic, common sense. You can't just run out into the dark."

"*Gringo!*" he muttered again.

"Here comes Peter," I commented. I was looking through one of the especially wide cracks in the back wall. "He went to bring up water for the tank, but it looks as if he forgot his bucket."

Kara was busy examining David's arm, so I went back out and met Peter on the porch. He was panting and his hair was falling over his forehead. "Marilyn," he exclaimed, "I met a couple Miyames on the path to the river – Chief Jaime and his son Misael. They killed a tapir early this morning. Before they cut it up, or whatever they want with it, you should come look."

"Is it very far?" I asked, glancing back towards the house.

He shook his head. "It's about halfway to the river," he answered. "I'm sure David wants to see it."

"Yes, and Sadie too," I said. "Can you call the children over here?"

As he ran towards the runway I ran back inside. "Come on, David," I said, grabbing his hand. "The Miyames killed your tapir."

Along with Kara, we met the others outside and then headed down the trail. Jake and Kara had seen several tapirs before, but our family and Peter hadn't. It was a couple minutes of walking, but David insisted that his pain was lessening.

"Here it is," Peter said. He was carrying Dennis on his shoulders and leading the way. Ahead of us was a large creature lying beside the path, and Chief Jaime and Misael, who were standing off to the side talking.

"*Hola,*" I greeted in Spanish. They glanced at me, and then continued their conversation in their strange, gurgling Miyame language. I turned away, a flush of crimson warming my face. Chief Jaime owed us his life and we had come to his home with the express purpose to help them. One would think he would at least be polite.

I looked down at the tapir. Its feet were like a pig's, only thicker and larger. The creature was huge. It was the size of a small pony, with tight, dark skin and a monstrous snout, and white-tipped ears. "It must be at least five hundred pounds," David guessed, giving the dead body a small kick. "Hmm, it's big."

"That is a huge one," Jake agreed.

"That's the thing that bit Daddy?" Sadie said with round eyes, looking up at me.

Jimmy looked alarmed. "It tried to eat Daddy?" I ruffled his hair comfortingly.

Peter turned to the two Miyames. "Thank you for letting us look at it," he said.

"Yes, thank you," David echoed. "Would you like to come visit our place sometime?"

Misael shot us a quick glance, but the chief didn't even look at us.

"Come on," I whispered. "Let's go home."

10

Snakebite!

Christmastime came and it was nothing like Christmas at home. Our small budget supplied by the MLA did not encourage us to buy any gifts. In fact, we hardly noted the holiday's passing. Anthony and Joyce called over the radio on New Year's Eve, thanking us for our perseverance on foreign shores and wishing everyone a fruitful year to come.

January came and went. I remember in February of that year, I began to develop a phobia of small wriggly creatures – only, in Colombia, they aren't really small. One morning I woke up later than usual; David was out front with the kids, and Peter was in Bogotá for the week.

I was sitting on the edge of my bed, pulling my socks on. I casually glanced to the side and my heart stopped. A large, hairy spider, almost the size of my hand, had just wriggled out from beneath the blanket. It stood poised at the edge of my bed, two of its legs in the air. I jumped to my feet and hopped across the room, pulling my denim jeans up as I reached the door. "David!" I hollered.

He came running up. I grabbed his hand and pointed him toward the bed, staying a cautious three feet away from it. As he pulled off his shoe and advanced, my eyes darted around the room, looking for every pile of clothes and piece of furniture a spider could possibly wriggle out of.

"There, it's dead." The spider was on the floor with its legs curled up. David picked it up gingerly and carried it out the door. The moment the creature was gone, I pulled all the sheets off my bed, vigilantly watching for any of its relatives. Then I began pulling the packing crates apart, stomping on a few smaller spiders I found.

"What are you doing?" Jimmy asked an hour later when he came inside. I had torn everything apart and was engaged in mopping the floor, ceiling and wall. I smiled at him grimly.

"I'm killing all the spiders and getting rid of their hiding places. They like piles of mucky laundry, and unwashed sheets, and dirty corners."

"Oh, good, I don't like spiders." He skipped over to the shelf and grabbed David's hammer. "Daddy said I could help him hammer some nails."

"Watch your fingers," I warned him.

David and Peter had cleared out a bit of jungle and were building a small wooden structure. It was behind our house, down a slight slope and to the right of the river trail. David intended to use it as an office and keep our important papers there, and it would also serve as Peter's house. Jake Perry had flown in with materials several times, and now they were on the last leg of its construction.

I watched Jimmy run out and then turned back to work. I had taken down the hammocks because they were in my way, but now I hung them back up. I then pushed the crates into the desk's corner, and the desk into the bed's corner. I surveyed my new arrangement and gave a sigh of satisfaction.

I found Sadie and enlisted her help in washing the sheets in a tub of river water with a bar of soap. After hanging them up to dry, I went back inside and wiped down the mud stove, and scrubbed the floor and wall around it. I tidied up the kitchen shelf and then wandered about the one-room house, looking for anything else to clean or organize. When the sheets were dry I made the bed and called my job complete.

The next morning I woke up especially early and saw a spider on the floor.

"David!" I grabbed his shoulder and shook him violently. "Another spider, it's a big one, kill it! Kill it!"

Mumbling incoherently, he got up and smashed it for me. He went outside and wiped it off his shoe. When he came back I was gazing at our home disconsolately, my fingers pressed against my temples. He put his hand on my shoulder.

"I'm sorry, Marilyn. There's always going to be spiders."

"No. There shouldn't be." My eyes swept across the room, but everything was clean and in order. "Where are they hiding? They can't hide anywhere. Where are they coming from?"

"Marilyn," he remonstrated, but I ignored him. I ran past the hammocks and peered under the shelf, and then looked accusingly at the desk. A glance under it produced nothing; it was spick and span, without so much as a crumb for a spider to hide behind. I ran to the front door, but it was too low down for such large spiders to fit under.

"This can't happen, David. I cleaned everything. Where are they coming in?"

He gave a wry smile and stuck his fingers through a crack in the door. "We can't keep them out, Marilyn."

I sighed and plunked down on the bed. "David, I don't like spiders."

He sat down beside me. "Nobody does."

"Except for Dennis. He likes poking them with sticks."

"Well, Dennis is a special child."

I leaned my head against his shoulder and yawned. "I change my mind; I'm not getting up early today. I'm going back to bed."

"I change my mind, too," David said, echoing my yawn. "I'm not getting up at all."

"David, Marilyn," we heard Peter's voice through the door. "Chief Jaime says he'll come tonight for a Bible study."

"Well, he's an early bird," David muttered.

"Did you talk with him just now?" I asked, sitting up.

"Yes," he answered. "I saw him walking across the runway toward the jungle, so I said good morning, and we talked a little."

So March 27, 1975 is the day he came. Chief Jaime showed up that evening with a handful of his relatives – his quiet wife, his youngest son, who was a shy, tiny boy named Juan, a couple older aunts, and an old man.

They all seemed like silent statues to me. We found very quickly that the three older people did not understand Spanish. The woman translated parts of David's Bible reading into the Miyame language, but my heart sank as I realized they weren't hearing enough to even understand.

We explained to Chief Jaime that we wanted to put these words into the language of his tribe. He nodded. "Like the other missionary, you want your book in our tongue," he said, referring to Jim Warden. "But I do not understand this book."

David jumped on the chance. "This is God's book," he said. "He is the greatest Chief of all, Chief over all chiefs – and he has a message for us. Do you want to understand?"

Chief Jaime thought for a moment. "It is late," he said at length. He said goodbye in the Miyame language and then rose to his feet. His relatives copied his farewell and then they left.

"Jim Warden sure didn't leave us an easy task," I muttered, tidying up. "These people are bent on not listening."

"We'll get through to them," said David. "With just a little more prayer and effort."

Inwardly I wondered just how much more prayer and effort was needed.

The following day Lucrecia came by with a gift of *casabe* bread. She didn't say much, and she left quickly. A full week went by without a word exchanged between us and the Miyames. It was a Thursday when we completed the construction on our little office-shed. There were a few finishing touches left, but we quickly moved the desk and our papers over.

"Look at the room we've cleared up," I said to David, looking at our house. The absence of the desk had a huge impact on our tiny space.

Peter walked in. "David," he said, "There are quite a few wooden planks left over, and some other things. Could I use a few? I promised your kids I'd help them make some sort of playhouse."

"Of course," answered David. "Where are you going to put it?"

"They want it down the trail towards the river," he answered. "I can't make a treehouse since none of the trees around here would work for that. It'll just be a little hut on the ground."

"All right, thank you Peter."

"Yes, thank you," I echoed. As Peter walked off I smiled at David. "The kids will love a playhouse. What a neat idea."

David shook his head. "Peter doesn't know how to build," he said. "He helped me with our shed, so I know that he's much better with a pen and paper or medical kit than with a hammer and nails."

I laughed. "Makes sense. You did construction back in the States, David. Peter only took a few classes at a mission camp. By the way, your shed is very impressive."

"Thanks. In a couple years, maybe I'll try building us a new house and we can use this one for storage."

Peter spent every spare moment building the hut. He would take

Jimmy or Sadie and sometimes Dennis and they'd go down the trail toward the river. Halfway between the water and the house was where he built it. A couple days after he started, I saw the project for the first time. Lunch was waiting, so I went down to fetch them.

Peter had said that he had built a hut like this before on a short-term missionary trip to Ecuador with his father. He had also learned a lot from David. Back in Washington, framing had been David's specific profession. As I walked up, I found Sadie and Jimmy pulling up ferns and tossing aside sticks, clearing around the half-built hut. "Hello Mama!" the kids called.

"It's lunch time," I announced. "Anybody hungry?"

"I am!" Jimmy threw down his armful of brush. I'll race you home, Sadie!"

Sadie set the stick in her hand by the unfinished hut, and brushed dirt off her overalls. "I'll be there first!"

The two ran off. I turned to Peter, who was rummaging through some brush. "Are you coming?"

He glanced up at me. "Yes, I'm just... looking for something."

I stepped closer. "What are you looking for?"

He ran his fingers through his dark hair. "David's hammer. I was using it and then tossed it aside. If this were Colorado, I would see it easily – but in this jungle, the ground seems to swallow everything up!"

I mirrored his nervous expression. "We'd better find it. David loves his tools."

Both of us had lost his tools before, so both of us had learned the hard way that he did not take very kindly to people who lost them. I pushed back a few stiff branches on a tall bush and peered beneath. It was hard to find the jungle floor, and even harder to find something on it. Peter was on his knees, feeling through some ferns. Suddenly he gave a cry and fell backwards.

"What's wrong?" I asked, jumping a little.

Peter was sprawled out on his side, clutching one hand with another. "I think I got cut on something, or bit."

"Let me see," I said.

He gave me his hand. There was already a dab of blood, oozing out of a little puncture, right between his two tallest fingers. Even with such a small injury, my squeamish stomach did a flip; between the fingers seemed a most uncomfortable place to get hurt. "I'm not sure what sort of cut it is," I said at last. "But it might have been a snake."

He shrugged. "There are lots of snakes out here that aren't poisonous, so unless I start reacting, I should be fine no matter what it was."

"Should we call Jake and ask him to bring Kara?" I asked anxiously.

He shook his head. "It doesn't really hurt – it was just sharp pain at first. It was probably just a jagged branch or sharp leaf. Let's go get lunch, Marilyn, I'll find the hammer when I come back."

We walked back up the trail. I made a mental note to keep Peter around the house for a little while and watch for any symptoms of poisonous snakebite, and to ask David what he thought. The children were sitting on the porch with their lunch, and I could see David on the runway talking with a passing Miyame, who was only talking out of civility.

I sank onto the porch and leaned my head against the railing. Today was especially warm, and the heat seemed to be draining my energy. My eyes followed Peter as he walked across the porch, went into the house, came out of the house; but he seemed to be moving painlessly. All the poisonous snakebites Anthony Carter had told us about had affected the victim quickly and noticeably. I finally took my eyes off him and focused on the little ones.

They were tired, so after they had finished eating I settled all four down for naps. After they drifted off to sleep, I stepped onto the front porch. David was sitting on one end, leaning against the railing, eating his lunch. Peter was on the steps, slouched forwards and rubbing his eyes. I sat down on the hammock and yawned.

"Tired, Marilyn?" asked David, glancing towards me.

I shook my head. "Not really. This warm air just makes me sleepy. Peter, are you alright?"

"Yes, I'm fine. I just feel a little drowsy."

I slid to my feet. "If you don't feel like walking all the way to your house, you can use this hammock," I suggested, jumping off.

He got up and climbed in. I sank down beside David and leaned my head back. "I wonder how everyone is doing back home," I said.

David took another bite, chewing slowly and thoughtfully. "I'm sure they're fine," he said at last. "Your brother's out of law school by now. My sis Linda is probably climbing the ladder in the MLA, before we know it she'll be its president."

"Meredith might've found a special man by now," I said, smiling at a cloud in the sky. "We've been gone for a year. She could be engaged and we wouldn't know it."

He nodded. He had stopped eating and his blue eyes were gazing into nothing, lost in thought. "Ma has a new rocking chair, I'm sure."

I glanced at him in surprise. "New rocking chair? Why would you say that?"

"Because I was always fixing it. The screws in the armrests come out sometimes, and the holes are worn out and too wide. And I'd always push the backrest back into place. If you applied too much pressure to it, it would just slip off. Ma's had that chair since I could remember. She used to rock me to sleep on it when I was little. The only reason she's kept it so long is because I begged her. But with me gone and it falling apart, she's probably got a pretty new one, made of dark wood, with a blue and green blanket draped over it. That's what she always wanted. Not the old knothole-spotted wood, with the red and white checkered cushion on top."

I laughed and squeezed his hand. "It's just a rocking chair, David."

"I know, but it's special. Don't you have anything special that you've had to say goodbye to?"

I thought for a moment. "There's my horse," I remembered, "That my parents bought me when I was eleven. He was a pretty gray gelding, and I named him Skeeter. He was sort of the color of a rainy sky in winter. I sold him when I married you. At that time in my life, it was the saddest thing that had ever happened to me." I sighed.

David squeezed my hand. "But it was worth it, wasn't it?" he asked softly. "The bond you and I share, the family we have – it makes it seem so small, doesn't it?"

"So what about leaving the rocking chair for Colombia?" I said.

Before he could answer, Sadie peeped out of the front door. "Mama, I left Daddy's water bottle by our hut. I'm really thirsty. Can I go grab it?"

"You all are leaving Daddy's things all over the place," I laughed, rising to my feet. David glanced at me and I quickly regretted what I said. "Sure, run grab it."

She thumped down the porch steps and disappeared down the trail. David was staring me down, waiting for an explanation. I sighed. "Peter lost your hammer earlier. Apparently he tossed it aside, and then couldn't find it again."

"He needs to stop using my things if he's going to lose them," said David, his voice getting heated. "He's worse than the kids. That hammer is a fundamental part of our survival out here, not a toy!"

From somewhere in the jungle thicket came a shriek. I spun around and hit my head on a porch beam, and then staggered down the steps. David, his eyes full of worry, raced past me. I pushed myself to keep up, and I could hear Peter behind me. We could hear Sadie screaming, over and over again.

David skidded to a stop and I nearly crashed into him. We had run down the trail, and now stood beside the children's hut. Sadie had stopped screaming, and was standing rigidly still with her little hands clutching her chubby cheeks. Her eyes were firmly fixed on the ground. David dropped onto one knee beside her.

"Sadie, are you all right? Are you hurt?"

She kept her face tilted downwards. "I'm fine," she said in a shaky voice, "I just got scared."

"Why, sweetie?" I asked, touching her curls. "What scared you?"

"It was a snake, Mama."

"Oh, but you're all right," David said, "There are lots of snakes out here. As long as you're not hurt, there's no need to scream."

Peter nodded. "Where did it go, Sadie? We can find it and kill it for you if it makes you feel better."

"I'm watching for it," she answered. "It went into the bush." We followed her gaze to the foliage right at her feet. David stood up slowly. We heard some rustling, and then suddenly it slid out. It was long, and striped with vibrant red, black and yellow. Its head nearly touched Sadie's feet. She gave another scream, and David jerked her back. We stared at it. The snake paused, its head poised in the air, and then slithered over a shiny hammer almost entirely hidden by deep grass.

"The hammer," Peter said. His voice sounded dry and weak. "That's your hammer, David."

"David, kill that thing," I said, my eyes fixed on it. Most of the snakes we ran into were dull colored and non-poisonous; I wasn't sure what type of snake this was, but the bright colors and stripes were alarming. "If that bites Sadie it might kill her."

Quickly David stepped on it. With one foot pinning it down behind the head, he stomped on it with the other, gave it a few thwacks with the hammer, and then ground its head into the dirt with his heel. As he stepped off, it went into dying convulsions, tossing and writhing. Its head was smashed and disfigured, and yet it kept moving. Sadie grabbed my hand and began crying.

"It's dead now," David assured her. "It's dead. Even though it keeps moving, it'll stop soon, and it can't bite you."

"David, I… need help," Peter said. His words were dry and slurred together, and he was bent forward, his hands on his knees to support himself.

My mind flashed back to the small puncture between his fingers. "David, I think he was bitten," I said, my words coming out in a jumble. "Earlier, he was looking for the hammer, we weren't sure what had happened, we never saw the snake… David, do something!"

David grabbed Peter and helped steady him. "Are you in pain? We need to know if you were really bit. What do you feel like?"

"I can't see right," he stuttered. He was having a difficult time forming his words. "My head hurts."

"You left your glasses on the porch, is that why?"

"No, I'm seeing double. My sight's all messed up." He blinked. His eyelids were heavy and his eyes were red. "I can't swallow. There's a lump in my throat that won't go down, and my neck hurts… the muscles in my neck, they hurt."

"Marilyn, run to the house and call Jake," David said. "He can come out and fly Peter to Bogotá. They'll have antivenin there. I'll help Peter to the porch. Sadie, bring the hammer and bottle." Although he was trying to keep a strong composure, I could tell he was frightened. Snakebites were a Colombian experience we had always meant to avoid. I could almost hear the "ignorant *gringos*" I knew David was saying in his head. I let go of my daughter's hand and rushed down the trail.

"Jake, Jake!" I shouted, pressing the transmitter button. Dennis raised his head from his hammock sleepily, and then laid back down. I bit the end of my braid. Jake was taking forever to answer. "Jake!" I yelled again.

"Marilyn, please follow the rules for this radio," came the German's voice. "Try again."

"Jake, I..."

"Marilyn, you've got to follow the rules. It helps keep things clear. Please say who you are and who you're calling when you use the radio."

I wanted to hit him over the head with something. Swallowing my anger, I took a deep breath and began again. "La Inez to pilot, we need an emergency lift."

"That's better. What happened?"

"Peter was bit by a snake an hour or two ago. It's really affecting him now."

"Why didn't you call sooner?"

"Because... we didn't know sooner! Please, just hurry!" I banged my head against the wall in frustration. "Hurry, Jake, or Peter might die."

"All right. I'm on my way. Pilot out."

11

Close to God

Dennis had sat up in his hammock again, and was now staring at me with large, unblinking eyes.

"Lie down and sleep," I said, straining to keep my voice calm. "And Mama will tell you when you can get up from your nap." Jimmy and Mary were still asleep, so after Dennis laid his head down I stepped onto the porch. David was just staggering into sight, Peter leaning heavily on his shoulder. Sadie walked behind them, gripping the hammer and water bottle.

I helped lay Peter out on the porch. His skin had changed to a pale, washed-out color. "He's got muscle paralysis or something like that," David panted.

I wanted to do something. I racked my mind, but I couldn't think of anything that would help. "David, what do we do for snakebite? Once I heard of wrapping up the wound area tightly to keep the poison from spreading, would that help?"

He shrugged. "I don't know."

I shook my head in exasperation. "We've got to do something besides wait."

David pushed open the door. "I'll talk to Kara. She might know something. You and Sadie watch him."

The door shut behind them, and I sank to my knees beside Peter. His face was ashen and his hands were clenched. He glanced at me and tried to smile, but his effort slipped away and was replaced by creases of pain. The absence of his glasses made him look strangely different. I twisted around to see behind me and saw the lenses, balanced on the railing beside his hammock.

"Please." Peter's voice made me turn back. His eyes were shut and he was breathing heavily. "Please, please tell me I won't die without doing something for Jesus."

Sadie looked at me and I opened my mouth to say something, but my tongue was dry, and my words were stuck in my throat. I shook my head. "You're not going to die," I said, managing a smile. "You couldn't have gotten too much venom. It's probably just enough to make you uncomfortable. You won't die."

"No, Marilyn, no... you know I might. I'm not afraid of dying, I'm just afraid of my life ending when I've hardly lived it. Do you know what I mean? It's... sort of like leaving a painting before it's finished, or, or, a book with empty pages."

"Peter, what matters is that you tried and did what God asked. You've done so much."

"Tell me," he said through teeth gritted in pain, "Tell me one thing I've done... just one soul who's been saved because of me, one life that's better because of me."

"That doesn't matter!" I cried, trying to flounder out of this nightmare. "We'll never know the full extent of how God has used us. It might be your death that serves as an example to others. God saves people, not us. It doesn't matter if you've managed to be the top Christian in our human eyes. Just live every moment you have for

God, whether it's a lifetime or just twenty years." I choked out the last words.

Tears were welling up in my eyes, blurring my vision. Peter should have been treated immediately after his bite. He was going to die, and be gone, forever. A wave of grief swept over me, and I broke down in sobs.

I felt David's arm slip around me, and a surge of warmth flooded through me. "There's nothing we can do, Kara says," he whispered. "God, he's in Your hands." I kept crying, but they weren't desperate tears; they were tears of sorrow mingled with surrender. And when you surrender your desperation to God, it doesn't necessarily lessen the pain; but it gives you something to hold onto. Like a life buoy thrown to a drowning man; he's still in the ocean, but he's safe.

It seems we spent an eternity on that porch. Clouds drifted by. Our watches ticked. All these things that happen every moment of our lives continued the same way they always had and always would. Every second that slipped by, life was happening. Our lives were frozen in a moment of time, but somewhere still, the river rippled, the trees grew, and the earth turned.

It seemed we were waking up to a new reality when the humming of Jake's airplane met our ears. David and I stood up and watched it touch the runway. As it slowed to a stop, we helped Peter to his feet and dragged him down the porch steps. I grabbed his glasses and carried them along. Kara came running out from the plane to help us, while Jake went behind the shed to fetch some more fuel. We reached the Cruiser, and David helped push Peter up and into the backseat. I stepped back, staggered, and nearly fell. Kara grabbed hold of me. "Let's go up to the house," she said.

She led me off the runway, and I clung to her. "I don't know what's wrong with me," I stammered shakily, "My heart's racing and I feel giddy. I don't know why. Kara, why do I feel so sick?"

"It's been a lot of excitement," she said, "You'll feel queasy for a little while."

I shook my head. "I didn't realize I was this spineless. It was like this with David and the tapir, too. Oh, what is wrong with me?"

We stepped into the house and she gave me a quick hug. "Calm down! You're fine. You're one of the strongest women I know. You just need to calm down. The sooner you forgive yourself for being weak the stronger you will be."

I couldn't see the logic in that, but I decided it was one of those things you had to be level-headed to understand. I sank onto the bed and mulled over my life. Unresponsive tribespeople... poisonous wild animals... and a German pilot who took forever to show up. It wasn't the glorious life of ministry I had always envisioned back in the States. I leaned back and covered my face with my hands.

"Marilyn, just trust God." Kara was busying herself about my house, tidying and arranging. "Whatever you're thinking, He's the answer."

Trust God. What did that mean? Yesterday I had trusted God; yesterday Peter hadn't been dying. I couldn't just let go of my fears, I was... too afraid to do that. How would trusting God help Peter now? It seemed there was no rhyme or reason to who died and who lived, it was as random as the flip of a coin. Forgetting my worry and trusting God almost seemed like shutting myself up in the closet ignoring the inevitable.

"What if Peter dies?" I asked.

"Then we still trust God," Kara answered firmly. "Right now we're standing at a door, and we don't know what's on the other side. But God does; he knows this house inside out, and better yet, he shaped it. And God loves Peter far more than we ever could."

"But how do I trust God? Is there some magic prayer of acceptance I should be saying or a special profound feeling I should get?"

Kara paused. "Marilyn, this isn't the best example, but imagine if David had absolute control over what happens in Peter's life – whether he lived or died. Would you be worried if Peter got bitten by a snake?"

"Yes, a little..."

"Of course. But would you follow David around, ask him what he's doing, and fret, and fret, and fret?"

"No, because David cares so much for Peter, he would know what he's doing."

"That's because you trust him. You know his heart and you know it is full of love, and he must have a plan. God orchestrates all of creation, so we've got to trust Him on a much larger scale. But He wants us to know His heart, and understand that it's full of love, and He has a plan. God loves Peter, and accepting that is trust. It's not getting a funny feeling and following your emotions – that's blind trust. It's understanding and knowing who God really is."

Basic concepts such as perseverance and trust were much deeper and yet much simpler than I had ever realized. A disturbing question rose in my mind. Was it the missionary life that had shown me all this? I grappled with the question. Would I have been exposed to the basic, raw truths of God in the same way if I had lived in Washington my whole life?

A few short minutes later, the plane buzzed off, carrying Jake, David, and Peter; Kara decided to stay with us, as there wasn't much she could do. She and I gathered the kids together and talked over the radio with Anthony and Joyce Carter before eating dinner. Dusk fell, bringing with it the sounds of jaguars, tapirs and other creatures roaming outside.

The next morning, we sat quietly in the house, waiting for a radio call from David. Even Dennis and Mary seemed to understand that something serious was happening, and they sat still. We knew the call would come, either with good news or with bad. I wondered what my reaction would be if Peter had died. Would I cry? Would I stare blankly at the wall? Would I start praying? *Now I'm overthinking it,* I thought. *Now I'll just be overly conscious of whatever I do.*

"Bogotá to La Inez," the radio crackled. It was David's voice. My stomach did a flip and I leaned closer.

"La Inez here," I said. My voice sounded strangely calm. It certainly didn't reflect the storm of emotions raging inside.

"I'm reporting on Peter Futterman," he said.

Yes, we know that, I thought.

David continued. "We got him to the compound at five forty-five last night, it took us a while to reach town but we found a hospital where a doctor was ready to treat him immediately. Pete was diagnosed with a definite snakebite, most likely coral, resulting in what the doctor called paralysis and respiratory failure. He got treated right away, and he's fine."

I stared blankly for a moment, and then a flood of tears overwhelmed my sight. *I was only supposed to cry if he died,* I thought, as I leaned my head against the radio. A laugh mingled with my tears. *Thank you, God. And thank you for how much you love us.*

"Marilyn," David said, and I lifted my head. "I love you, Marilyn. That was a scare, but he's alright. Praise God."

Peter came home the day after. His hair was immaculate and he wore his glasses, along with that laid-back expression he always had on his face. As he stepped out of the plane he was enveloped in hugs from me and the children. David also got his share.

We walked up to the house, and Kara and Jake joined us for dinner. As we all munched and chatted, I couldn't help but glance at Peter repeatedly. Here he was, fresh and ready as usual, when last I saw him he was dying without his glasses. God must have work for him yet. In a way, he was very much the little brother David and I never had.

"Are you going to finish the playhouse?" Jake asked, after we had recounted in detail the events leading up to Peter's bite.

Peter nodded. "I don't see why not. I'll clear the brush around it, so the kids won't be running into snakes."

"Everything seems to grow overnight here, though," David said. "I hacked another trail to the river with my machete just a week or two ago, I can't even find it now."

"The hut's right on our regular trail, so we'll have our eyes on it every day," I said. "We'll cut things down as necessary."

"Can you really get rid of the snakes?" asked Sadie.

"Of course, Sadie," I said. "We'll cut the grass, so there's nowhere for the snakes to hide. They won't like that, and they'll stay away. And remember, I was going to give you a box and a sheet for a table and a tablecloth, and you were going to keep your picture books in there."

"And can we have picnics next to it? With Daddy and Peter and everyone?" piped up Jimmy.

I smiled. "Yes, we'll have picnics," I said, "With Daddy and Peter and everyone."

12

The Hungry River

That hut was ill-fated from its beginning. It met its end in May 1975; the day is forever seared on my memory. It was a long, hard year for us, a year of spinning our wheels in the dirt and getting nowhere. We were without grip or tread in this tribe, and the most memorable events of that year were mishaps and calamities.

The weather had for once aligned with what we were used to in Washington; rain in Spring. The day the hut was destroyed I was trying to make *casabe* bread like the Miyames did, with little success. The older children had asked to play in their hut and I had granted permission. It was raining outside, but it had been for days and we were used to it. David was at the Perrys' place, helping Jake build an addition to his shed. I blamed my failed baking on his absence. Nothing went right when David was gone.

Mary was asleep in a hammock. Peter was on a chair, flipping through sheets of paper. He had brought our bits of translated verses in from the shed and was running through them, checking some words. When we were done with a book of the Bible, a translation consultant would go through it with us and check the accuracy. Jim Warden had done several books; we had done a piece of John. Most of our knowledge of the Miyame language came from Warden's charts rather than the Miyames themselves, so we couldn't be sure we had their grammar structure right.

I gave up on the bread and plunked down on a chair, despondent. The rain was gaining intensity, splashing against the roof. There was never any wind around our house, so the cracks in our walls posed no problem for rain getting in.

"The children should probably come in now," I thought out loud. "They're bound to be soaked."

Peter began tapping on the desk with his pen. "I wonder what all this rain has done to the river. It's probably risen quite a bit."

"I don't know, I haven't seen it in a while. Which reminds me, I haven't done laundry for a week." I sighed and closed my eyes. All was silent for a few moments, except the pattering of the rain and the steady *tap-tap-tap* of Peter's pen.

"Arturo told me that the river rises rapidly sometimes," Peter said, gazing at the ceiling. "And it'll lower just as fast. He said that jungle rivers are quite unpredictable, and over the years will change positions. Apparently a few years ago, the river bed was in a different place than it is now."

"Do you think it could shift closer to our house?" I asked. The *tap-tap* of his pen continued.

Peter shrugged. "I don't think so. The chief built his house here, and he should know the safe distance from the river."

We went quiet again. His pen continued tapping. The water continued drumming against our ceiling. I tried rocking my chair on its legs, and nearly tipped over. I had never thought I would crave a rocking chair as a missionary, but here I was. I thought of Olivia Cole's chair with the red and white checkered cushion that meant so much to David.

"Have you seen my watch?" Peter asked. He sounded tired. "Jimmy asked if he could wear it, so I let him borrow it. That was yesterday."

"Hopefully it's not lying in the mud getting rained on somewhere," I said. The sound of rain always made me drowsy. When mixed with a warm day, it was the recipe for a nap. "You don't need to let my children borrow your things."

"I don't mind it, as long as they return them."

Tap-tap-tap-tap. His pen continued a steady beat. "Marilyn, do you want me to help you bring the kids back?"

"Yes, thank you, Peter. They're bound to be getting wet."

I made no movement to get up. Going out in the rain did not sound appealing. I began to hope the kids would come in on their own.

"I wonder when David will be back," I said.

Tap-tap-tap-tap.

"Jake said maybe when there's a lull in the rain," Peter answered.

Tap-tap-tap-tap.

"He can fly in the rain, I've seen him do it before."

Tap-tap-tap-tap.

"I think they're waiting for a dry day to put some sealant on the shed, and then Jake will fly him back straight away."

Tap-tap-tap-tap.

"Would you quit that?" I sat up, opening my eyes and shaking my head. Peter paused, his pen poised in the air. "We've got to go get the kids. Can't you hear the rain? It's pouring out there, and they have Dennis with them."

He dropped his pen and stretched. "I suppose we'd better go."

I grabbed my poncho and opened the door. Pools of water were scattered about the clearing, and the runway had turned into a muddy stream. I pulled my hood over my hair and stepped out, Peter following. We were immediately drenched. As I ran towards the trail, splashing through the new landscape of small rivulets and ponds, I could hear the river. Normally I couldn't hear it until halfway down the trail. I pushed forward and tried to remember: how long had the kids been out here? I had let them out after lunch. My *casabe* bread was for dinner, and if I hadn't ruined it, it would have been ready by now.

Water dripped down the front of my hood into my face. As I slipped down the muddy trail I listened for my children's voices. I could only hear the river, but not its usual bubbling sound. Slowly it grew louder. It was rushing, crashing, thundering. It sounded so different than usual that I began to panic.

"Marilyn, it's flooding bad out here!" Peter shouted over the din. "It wasn't anything like this an hour ago."

I took another step and my boot sank six inches. Quickly I tilted my heel down and my toes up, anchoring my foot in my boot, and then I tugged. The water rushed close to the opening; desperately I pulled harder before the deluge poured in. At last it slipped free and I scrambled forwards to a place that looked less muddy. It wasn't any less wet though. There was standing water everywhere I looked. It was rising around the bushes and trees, wrapping everything in a soppy embrace.

"Peter, where is the hut?" I cried. Tears mingled with the raindrops on my face.

He pushed past me. "It should be a little further. Come on."

I stumbled after him. I gave up trying to keep the water out of my boots; within seconds my socks were drenched. The rain was pelting down on my head, my shoulders, the trees and splashing onto the ground around me. The water was falling down from above and rising below. Never before had I felt so trapped. And amid it all the river continued its persistent roar.

"This tree shouldn't be here," Peter said, grabbing onto a branch to steady himself. "This is all wrong. The water is washing our trail away and confusing us. We've been diverted off into the jungle."

"Peter, where are my children?" I wailed.

The rain in our eyes made it hard to see. He staggered to the left and blundered into some unyielding ferns. Pulling himself up, he sloshed past the ferns and I followed. "I think this is the trail," he shouted.

We waded down the path which had now turned into a stream. It reminded me of the creek behind my aunt's house. In summer, wearing t-shirts and shorts, Steven, Meredith and I would kick our sandals off and wade downstream. Sometimes the ground beneath our feet would sink downwards and the water would reach our knees, while at other points it would be shallower, and only to our ankles. The trail Peter and I were on did the same thing: it would dip lower and then climb higher.

Those summer afternoons seemed so far away. We would hold Meredith's hands because she was afraid of the water, and wave at any neighbors on the shore we saw passing by. We would play a game: the first person to fall and get wet, lost. Anytime the bank rose several feet higher than the water we would steer clear from it. They caved in sometimes, our aunt warned us, and we didn't want to be buried beneath the landslide. The sun would burn my nose and warm my ears, while my toes would wrinkle in the cool water the same way they did when I took a bath.

Sometimes we would take our aunt's rowboat upstream. The water was deeper that direction so we wouldn't get caught on rocks. Steven would insist on rowing all by himself until he got tired, and then he would refuse to do anything. Mom never came with us, and if we were away from her for more than ten minutes Meredith would start crying and would beg us to take her back. Steven would call her names, but he'd still always listen. Dad came with us one time, and even he was unable to console Meredith when she became desperate for Mom.

"Marilyn!" Peter shouted. His eyes were fixed on something down the trail.

With a start I awoke from my trance. The mighty, angry river stretched before us, eating away the land and pulling up huge trees, sweeping everything down river. It was swollen and raging, and had climbed up towards the house, swallowing everything in its way. Near the edge of the bank was a little brown smudge. I blinked water out my eyes and squinted. My heart skipped a beat as the smudge formed into a small hut with the swirling, frothing water reaching for it.

"Sadie!" Peter shouted, dashing towards it. His boots kicked up sprays of water. "Sadie, are you there?"

I ran after him, slipping over roots and stones hidden under the flood. The river was overrunning its new bed and with the help of the rain it was flooding everything. As I reached the hut, Peter was pushing on the door. "Open it," I shouted, my voice sounding weak against the crashing of the river. "Open it, Peter!"

He pushed his shoulder against it and shoved, but it didn't budge. I knew there wasn't a lock, or even a handle. Peter's building skills were few and inexpert. The hut could barely hold itself together, but somehow the door stayed shut as if it were latched. Taking a step back Peter lunged forwards, his shoulder hitting the door and crashing it open.

Bending over to get past the low-hanging door, we charged in and both tripped over a large, heavy crate. The children used it for a table, but now the door was in splintered fragments around it. My eyes swept the small, dark room, which smelled dank with water and mud. In one corner, little eyes blinked and peered at us. "Mama?" came Sadie's voice.

She and Dennis were huddled together, soaked and scared. As soon as they realized it was me, they rushed over and threw themselves into my arms. But there was no time for hugs.

"Where's Jimmy?" I asked.

"He went to get you," Sadie said, her blue eyes widening with fright. "Dennis was too scared to go through the water, so we waited here. I pushed the table against the door to keep the water out. I thought Jimmy reached the house."

My heart sank. "Let's get these two to the house," Peter said, "And then we'll look for Jimmy." I nodded, and we all struggled out the small door. The water was threatening to reach Sadie's knees, but she fought her way along bravely. My hood had slipped off, and water was cascading down my back and my face. I coughed and shivered. The air was relatively warm, but being submerged in this manner was enough to chill anyone.

We made it quite a way down the trail when Peter set Dennis down. The water wasn't as high this near to the house, and he was able to stand on his own. "I'll look for Jimmy," Peter said, "You get them to the house."

He splashed off, and I took Dennis's hand. "Let's pretend we're river-walking," I said, raising my voice so they could hear me, "And we don't want to fall down and get wet, so walk steady."

"I'm already wet," Sadie whimpered.

"Be a big girl for Mama and pretend," I said. "The first person to fall down loses the game." I placed Dennis's fingers in one of my jeans pockets, and Sadie's in another. "Hold on there," I instructed, "And don't let go, just follow Mama."

Step by step, we inched closer to home. My bones were beginning to ache and my sides hurt, but I tried to ignore the sensations. I concentrated on the slight tug of my children holding onto my jeans, making sure I didn't lose that feeling. Right now, it was the only feeling that mattered. The ground was sloping upwards and the water was lowering, and after a couple minutes of sludge and water the dim outline of the house stood out against the dusk. "First person to the house wins the game," I panted.

Sadie and Dennis both broke free and rushed on. I jogged after them, putting my last bit of energy into this last stretch. As we stumbled up the porch steps, I inaudibly thanked God for stairs rather than a ladder.

We sank down on the floor just inside the door. Mary in her hammock didn't even wake up. We were all a muddy, sopping mess; my boots were full of water. But we were too exhausted to care. When the sun came out, I could clean up all the mud and wash all the clothes. Worrying about that could wait. As long as we were alive, I could always clean things up later.

"La Inez, are you there? Marilyn?" David's voice came over the radio and my heart gave a leap. Sliding the muddy kids off my lap, I fumbled with the radio's buttons.

"David, I'm here," I said, forgetting all radio protocol.

"Marilyn, are you alright? I've been calling every ten minutes and you haven't answered. There's bad flooding here, and Jake said it must be even worse over there."

"It's horrible, David. We've lost Jimmy and Peter is looking for him. The river has risen up to where the kids' hut is, everything up to that point is washed away. All the puddles around our clearing are joining together and turning into standing water."

"Oh, Marilyn! Are Dennis and the girls safe?"

"Yes, I have them here. We're exhausted, David, and I'm so worried for Jimmy."

"Marilyn, how does the runway look?" interrupted Jake's voice.

"It's flooded, that's for sure."

"But how bad? Is it water, or mud? Soft ground is what I have to avoid."

"I don't know, it looks a mess. It and the office shed are on lower ground than the house, and there's water up here. David, I'm afraid the river is going to tear its way up here and wash away the house."

"If that happens, go to the Miyames," said David. "One of their *malokas* in the jungle should keep you safe."

"All right, I will. Are you going to try to come out here?"

"I will," Jake said hesitantly, "But I'm not sure if I can land. I'll come out and take a look at it."

"Thank you, Jake."

"I love you, Marilyn," David said, "Keep yourself and the kids safe. I'm praying. Over and out."

13

Letter From Home

I was amazed with the power of the river. It had always looked like harmless, green, murky water, meandering down its course. But it had risen with greater strength than I had ever imagined. Anthony Carter had told us a story of flooding that had taken place in Ecuador a couple decades before, tearing away the ground with the missionaries' buildings – schoolhouse, clinic, huts. It had washed away years of hard work.

I was musing on these things as I cuddled with my children. After a few minutes I must've fallen asleep, because the next thing I knew Dennis was tugging on my hair. "The plane, Mama," he lisped, "I hear the plane."

I could hear it now too; the hum of Jake's engine, barely audible over the pouring rain. I pulled my wet boots over my damp jeans and ran outside.

The Piper Cruiser was flying in circles around the runway, like a bird in the sky. I watched as it made an especially low swoop, nearly touching the ground. I ran through the rain, getting drenched all over again, waving my hands and breathing in quick, excited gasps. David and Jake were on that plane, and they could find my son.

The plane made one last circle, and then pointed its nose towards the sky. I waited expectantly for it to dive down again, but it didn't. Instead it swung off over the trees. I listened to its buzz die away. Now I was left with only the sound of the rain. I kicked the stream of water around my legs, and then raced back to the house.

"Pilot to La Inez," I heard Jake say. I sat down by the radio.

"La Inez here. Jake, how could you leave?"

"I can't land on that runway. My wheels would touch the ground unevenly, I could get stuck in that mud. I once saw a Cruiser like mine try to land in mud, and its nose sunk, it flipped and wrecked the engine and killed the pilot."

"Jake, you need to land. My son could be dead."

"We would be, too," he said. There was a moment of silence. "How many people do you want to lose today?"

I buried my face in my hands and cried. "Help us, God," I sobbed.

We were left alone again. The rain beat against the house and I knew the water was rising. The river could wash away our house, office shed, outhouse and runway, taking us with it. I tried to pray, but I could only cry. A verse I had memorized suddenly came to mind. *Likewise, the Spirit also helpeth our infirmities: for we know not what we should pray for as we ought: but the Spirit itself maketh intercession for us with groanings which cannot be uttered.* I tried to remember the reference but it escaped my memory. I began whispering the verse to myself repeatedly.

"Marilyn," I heard David on the radio.

"Yes?" I sniffled.

"Marilyn, you..."

The door opened and a frightened little boy tumbled in. "Jimmy!" I exclaimed. Peter came in too, but my eyes were on my son. "David, Jimmy's here and safe."

"Marilyn," Peter said, grabbing my shoulder. He hardly looked like himself. His clothes were sopping wet and his hair was matted to his forehead. "Marilyn, the shed."

"Jimmy's safe?" David came over the radio. "Praise God."

"What about the shed?" I said. My finger was subconsciously on the transmitting button.

"It's gone," he said. "The whole slope over there up to the runway is gone."

A tremor of shock passed through me. "The desk, the new cabinet, Peter..."

"It's all gone," he said.

I let go of the radio. The world went silent.

Voices, rain and other noises seemed to evaporate. The wall was swimming in front of my eyes. Besides a couple papers Peter had taken out, all of our translation work as well as Jim Warden's had been washed away with the office shed.

I placed a hand on the wall to steady myself as David's voice drifted into my awareness. "Just keep an eye on the river, Marilyn." His voice was hollow. "As long as it doesn't reach the house, you're safe. Don't worry about anything else. Just keep yourself and the kids high and dry."

Dry seemed a word of the past. "I will," I breathed quietly. "I love you."

"Love you too," he said.

I held Jimmy close and we both dozed off. It was an uneasy sleep for me; I woke up every few minutes and peeked out the front door to check on the river. Pretty quickly it was too dark to see. At last I fell into a deep sleep. Sometime during the night the rain stopped. When we woke up the next morning, the water was slowly but surely subsiding.

I stood on the front porch and breathed in deeply. Several hours had been devoted to sleeping, that blissful task making us oblivious to pain and duty and worry. But one thing I've discovered is that we can't sleep forever. I began walking down the stairs.

I sat down on the bottom step. A small, still puddle lay at my feet, with myself and my world reflected in it, upside down and rippled. There was no sky, only trees with patches of a strange gray that wrapped the clearing in a damp bubble. *This is why we left, Steven,* I heard a voice in my head saying. *We left to toil in a place where a little rain could wash away everything – everything.* Purpose lay wasted in the silt beneath the puddle.

Pressing my lips together, I rose to my feet and walked through it, splashing droplets over my fresh skirt. My heart was pumping feebly and my hands were shaking, but I ignored the sensations and crossed the clearing. I needed to check the runway. I needed to look for the chickens. I needed to make sure my kids kept their clothes clean and stayed out of the mud. I could not sit and listen to the silence.

That day passed by slowly. Jake still couldn't land so we were on our own. Instead of clear sunshine to warm the waterlogged area, it was a typical jungle day: warm and steamy. But *steamy* was taken to a whole new level. As all the water evaporated, the air grew heavy and moist. Everything in the house grew damp. Nothing would dry. The fresh clothes I had put on my children were damp and uncomfortable.

I spent the day cleaning mud out of the house. The children played on the porch, since the ground was too wet and loose for me to allow them any further. Peter went down the trail and checked on the river. He came back up with a grim face.

"It took a lot of trees down, and the whole place looks different," he informed me. "The little hut is gone. It must have been washed away shortly after we found the kids."

I was picking up the children's muddy clothes scattered about the floor. I wanted to ask about the office shed and make sure I hadn't been dreaming the day before, but I knew I hadn't, and I couldn't bear to talk of it. I shook Jimmy's jeans and something clattered to the ground.

I bent down and picked it up. "It's your watch, Peter."

He took it and smiled. I continued throwing the dirty clothes into a bucket in the corner. Why smile? Why care? I would've given my watch and my right arm with it to bring back our Miyame Bible. Peter walked outside but came back in a few minutes later.

"The chickens are gone," he said.

"Don't point it out to the kids," I replied listlessly, "until David gets home."

A touch of resentment seeped into my thoughts. *Thanks, David, for being gone,* I thought.

Night rolled in and we climbed into the bed and hammocks, damp but clean. Early the next morning Jake called, asking about the runway. Since our clearing was on relatively high ground, it had drained quickly. It looked a little rougher and rutted than it had before, but it was usable.

We were all standing outside waiting when the plane landed. As the engine shut off, I walked over to it, holding Mary. I watched as David stepped out and turned towards me. His blue eyes were vivid with both fear and pain. I knew I should hug him, encourage him, tell him we were all right and that we forgave him for not being there, that God had a plan despite the horrible things he let happen to us... but I did none of these. I simply gave him a little nod when his eyes met mine.

He didn't come near me. Only Kara did; she threw her arms around me and squeezed. "Hello, Marilyn!" she greeted. "We flew into Bogotá yesterday, and the Carters supplied us with some blankets and sheets, as well as tools. David said he was keeping some of his tools in the shed you lost."

"Thanks," I said.

Jake was puttering off to get some fuel like he always did. Kara was bustling about, checking on my children and asking what my plans were for dinner. Even David was mechanically unloading the supplies, in want of something better to do. I wanted to hit somebody, anybody, for acting so normal. I wanted to see somebody feel as horrible as I did.

David stopped about an arm's distance from me and dropped a heavy box onto the ground. He reached into his coat pocket. "Anthony gave this to me while we were in Bogotá," he said, holding out an envelope. "A letter from Linda. I haven't opened it yet, I thought I should wait until you and I could read it together."

"You shouldn't let that box sit in the mud," I said.

He looked at me a moment, nodded, and then picked it up and walked away. I fingered the envelope and gazed after him.

"I bought a pork roast in Bogotá," Kara said, patting my shoulder. I shrank away from her touch. "I think I can manage cooking it in your oven. I'll go put it in."

Peter glanced at me, then at Kara, and then shifted his glasses. "Thank you," he said. "I can help you start it. You've got an actual stove at your place, so you probably don't know how to use ours."

Kara and Peter headed towards the house. I felt someone tugging on my sleeve.

"What is it, Jimmy?"

"Where did our chickens go?"

I looked up and my eyes met David's. I shook my head, and he immediately caught on. "Something very sad happened," he said.

Jimmy's lip trembled.

David's reaction caught me off guard. His eyes glistened with tears. He tried to smile, but the grief and disappointment hidden in his heart showed clearly on his face. He knelt down and laid his hands on Jimmy's shoulders.

"They moved," he choked out. He breathed in deeply and tried again more calmly. "The chickens moved away. They wanted to know what California was like. Do you know where California is?"

"Is it one of the States?" queried Jimmy's small voice.

"Yes, yes," David nodded. "We won't see them again, but..." his voice wavered again. "But I'm sure they're enjoying their new home. We'll get new chickens."

"Can you get six this time?" asked Jimmy. "One for each of us? So we can all name one?"

"I'll get six, I promise."

After the plane was unloaded, I wandered onto the porch and sank into the hammock. David followed me and gestured towards the letter in my hand. "It smells like lavender," he said lamely. "Linda's letters always smell like flowers and things."

I handed it to him. "You should read it."

He pulled out the letter and scanned over the contents. "Doesn't say much," he said. "A bit of MLA info at the top. She mentions that conference in Bogotá coming up next month that the Carters were telling us about... she mentions our furlough. They come every five years, remember, but she says here that for every injury or unexpected calamity," his voice wavered, "they knock off some time. They had it scheduled for the year after next, but after what happened I think they'll move it sooner."

"Not soon enough," I commented. "Is that all?"

"A lot of Bible verses," he said. "That's how Linda fills her letters – she covers the page with verses. I used to do that when Mom made me send letters to my grandparents, but that was only because I could never think of what to say and I had to fill space."

"You did that with every letter you wrote me when we were engaged," I reminded him. "You're terrible at writing letters. You'd almost gone through the entire Bible by the time we got married."

"We'll read the verses she sent aloud during dinner," David said. "There's something else here at the bottom. She wrote something about your brother!" He paused, and I could see his eyes slowly going over the words.

"What does it say?" I asked.

"Shh, I'm trying to read."

"Read it aloud!"

He ignored me and kept his nose buried in the paper. I knew that despite being a linguist, he had never enjoyed reading aloud. I waited anxiously, wondering if I should be excited or frightened to hear the news. At last, David looked up at me with a wide grin and I relaxed. This would be the first good news I'd heard in a while.

"He's coming down to visit us!" David exclaimed.

I think I nearly fainted. Whatever I did, I flipped the hammock and found myself sprawled out on my back underneath it. David dropped to his knees beside me in concern. "Marilyn, what's wrong?"

"What's wrong?" I spluttered. "My brother is the most cynical man you'll ever meet, and he wants to see how we're doing. It would be hard enough to convince your mission-minded sister that we aren't wasting our time here, but my brother? What are we going to do?"

"It'll be fine," he assured me. "It'll be at least half a year before he makes it down here. And I'm sure your brother will have a change of heart if he sees how hard we try."

"Sees how hard we try? I sit a couple times a week with the women in the yuca fields or their *malokas*, and I read the Bible to them and they ignore me. You follow the men around as they fish and hunt and you preach salvation, and they ignore you. What is the use of trying? We translate the Bible and God washes it away! My brother will condemn our entire mission!"

"Well, let him!" David shouted back. He dropped my hand and rose to his feet. "Let him, Marilyn! I don't care what he says. If he thinks we've gone mad, let him say it!"

He stormed into the house, leaving me on the ground.

Half an hour later, somehow, we sat down for dinner. As the meal wound down, David quietly told the Perrys and Peter about Linda's letter, and I cringed as he mentioned Steven's anticipated visit.

"It'll be so exciting to meet your brother, Marilyn," exclaimed Kara, "Is he interested in mission work?"

"No," I said. I wanted to squirm like I did when I was younger, whenever I had a guilty conscience and my Dad was interrogating me. I cleared my throat. "No, he's a lawyer."

"Linda wrote some verses in her letter," David said, smoothing the paper out on the table. I hadn't exchanged a word with him since his outburst. Never before had I seen David display such a range of emotions as I had that day. "Jake, could you read them aloud for us?"

Without question Jake took the letter. "'Trust in the Lord with all thine heart; and lean not on thy own understanding. In all thy ways acknowledge Him, and He shall direct thy paths. Be not wise in thine own eyes: fear the Lord, and depart from evil. It shall be health to thy navel, and marrow to thy bones. Honor the Lord thy substance, and with the first fruits of all thine increase: so shall thy barns be filled with plenty, and thy presses shall burst out with new wine."

"That's in Proverbs three, isn't it?" Peter asked.

"Yes," Jake answered, leaning back in his chair. "I remember memorizing that shortly after I became a Christian. Trust in God's infinite wisdom, and not my limited understanding. Valuable lesson. It sure is a load off one's shoulders when you let God direct your path."

Kara nodded. "And like the verse says, it does wonders to the overall health and happiness of your life. Piling up stress will only weigh you down. If you hold onto each and every bad thing that happens, all with your own understanding... you're going to get bogged down with life."

I thought of my own life. At this point, it seemed to be rather bogged down. Jim Warden's nasty words, Peter's snakebite, the flood... I shuddered. I had wanted so badly to trust God, but it was so hard. Every time I was doing good in my Christian life I was tripped up. Would I ever get it right? Could I ever get it right?

That night, when the kids were asleep in their hammocks, I sat down on the bed with my Bible. Without thinking I opened it, as I did every night. I flipped through the pages, looking for the chapter in Judges I had read the night before. I began dragging myself through the story of Gideon. David was sitting on the bed next to me, his legs drawn up in front of him and his arms on his knees. He was staring at nothing, lost in thought.

I had never understood why Gideon had chosen a miracle with an old fleece of all things. Why not a bolt of thunder, fire on the sea, or a light show with the stars? "I gave Jake our registration letter for the Bogotá conference," I said, snapping the book shut and looking up. "He'll give it to Anthony. Now they're expecting us to show up."

"Marilyn," David said, his eyes still staring, "Do you want to go home?"

My eyebrows rose in surprise. Yes, of course I did, but I had never considered it an option, so I hadn't dwelt on the idea too much. I shrugged and tried to not sound so eager. "I do miss Mom and Dad, and Meredith and Steven, and my church, and my friends, and our old home. That was a pretty little house."

"We can go back," David said. He corrected himself quickly, shooting a glance at me. "We're not going to, but there's always a way to back out of this. We could go home and wait a few years until we're older and we understand what we're doing."

I nodded, getting up and setting the Bible on the shelf. "Do you want to go home, David?"

"Oh, no. I mean, I miss Linda, and my Ma. She's definitely gotten rid of her old rocking chair by now. I wonder if the people back home realize how important even little things like that become when you're in a jungle."

"Many things change when you're in a jungle," I said.

"Yes," he said.

We went silent. As I pulled the covers up, my heart was aching. David was homesick. A sense of insecurity reinforced the pain in my heart. Where was home? Our pretty little house belonged to someone else now. So did our car. Even the rocking chair was gone.

14

Higher Ground

Two-year old Dennis was snoring in my lap. How could he fall asleep so fast when it was so hot? We were in Anthony's pickup, and all of the windows were either open or missing, but even the flow of air wasn't enough to cool me down. Having a sweaty, heavy boy slumped over me didn't help.

We were on our way to the MLA conference in Bogotá. All of the MLA's missionaries in the area were attending, and a couple from a few other groups. We were meeting at a little church in town. I was riding in the cab where Anthony was driving, and Joyce was squashed between us. David and Peter had three kids with them in the bed of the truck. I wanted to be excited for the conference, but I had a vague feeling of uneasiness. I would've been more comfortable a year ago when things were looking bright. Or perhaps a year from now, we would be more successful. But at this moment in my life, I wasn't sure if I would enjoy what I envisioned as a meeting of missionaries swapping success stories, success formulas and success admiration.

The truck pulled off the paved road onto a strip of dirt beside the church. An old bus had rolled right up to the steps of the building, and several people were unloading. I pushed open my door and set Dennis on the ground and then slid out myself. An acrid smell of bad fuel coming from the bus hit my nose and I almost gagged. Its tires squealed and it rumbled away, while its former passengers entered the church.

The Carters, Peter, David, our kids and I made our way up the steps and into the sanctuary. "This is a Catholic church building," Anthony explained, "Built by their missionaries many years ago. This place is better for our meeting than the compound. The deacon is a kind man and a friend, so despite the animosity between our religions, he has allowed us to use this church."

I glanced around at our venue. There was a single aisle with pews lined up on either side, each with a hymnbook. Images of the saints crafted out of painted clay were hung on the walls. Down at the end of the room was the stage, which was elevated by one step. There was a table with a white cloth draped over it and two candles. A picture of the Lord's Supper was propped up in front of it. Behind all this were a few more candles, a few more images of the saints, with flowers mingled with it all, and above everything hung a crucifix.

Electric lamps hung down from the ceiling. They looked like lanterns to me, and they beamed a wonderful yellow light on the heads of the people below. There were two windows on either wall, and while each was tall and clear and let in plenty of light, the electric lights gave a more elegant feel to this tiny church. It was both sophisticated and homey. It was a difficult mix to pull off, but this little Catholic church did it very nicely.

I shuffled the kids into the back row and sat down next to them, pulling Mary into my lap. Anthony was introducing David and Peter to some other men. A mild-faced girl was at the piano, playing a gentle tune. Several women were grouped nearby, chatting. These missionaries had met each other during past conferences, and some lived in neighboring villages and saw each other regularly. Some were from Venezuela and one from distant Guyana. A few of the couples and families had been here in Colombia for years – some for over a decade. They knew Colombia and its people better than I did. I was beginning to question if I knew anything about Colombia at all.

I heard Kara's cheerful voice, and I stood up on tip-toe to see over some heads. The Perrys had just entered, and the Carters were greeting them. A man in a pressed suit leaned into the group and whispered something to Anthony. He nodded, and the two men headed down the aisle. I slid back into my seat and Mary crawled back into my lap. As Anthony and the man in the suit stepped onto the stage, everybody scrambled for a pew.

Even from the back I could see Anthony's blue eyes twinkling with pride at the congregation. "Good morning, friends, and thank you for coming," he began, all in English, which was odd to hear. "Compared to other gatherings, we are a small group, but a great work. Some of us work with mountain Indians, some in the lowlands. Some of us are in the jungle on branches of the Meta River. We are all on God's campus, teaching, as well as learning. For our faith is just as important to God as is the peoples' we serve."

There was a murmur of agreement, and then Anthony continued. "This is Micah Hale, from the southern Andes Mountains, as some of you know. Recently he preached a sermon to his congregation, and several were saved after hearing the Word. Micah brought his notes along with him, and he has agreed to preach on the same text to open up our conference."

"Yes, yes," said the man in the suit. "Praise the Lord. He is doing a great work among the heathens of this country. Yes, many Indians have been converted in the lower Andes. The thirsty have found their drink, the hungry their food, and the weary their rest. And we shall continue to care for the needy people of this country, yes, shall we not?"

Another murmur of agreement. Anthony's tanned face creased into a smile. "Yes, we shall. Micah is also going to lead us in a few songs. Miss Palmer will accompany us at the piano."

"In your pews you will find hymnals that Mr. Carter has brought," Micah directed. "Please, take one and turn to page one hundred twenty-three. Please stand as we sing, yes, yes."

"One two three," David whispered to Sadie, who was flipping through our hymnal. "No, forwards – you missed it – one two four, one two three, good job."

The mild-faced girl played a soft introduction, and then we sang. "Sing the wondrous love of Jesus; sing His mercy and His grace..." Dennis was sitting down out of my sight, but I could sense he was fidgeting. Mary was beginning to squirm in an unrelenting, flopping way, and I had to either set her down or drop her. The moment I placed her on the seat her foot touched Dennis's, and he kicked her. She gave an indignant cry and kicked him back.

"I think I have to step outside with the kids," I whispered into David's ear. I was wondering how he had ended up on my left with Sadie, while all the younger kids were on my right. He was getting off easy today.

"Oh no, they're fine," he whispered back.

Do you want to trade seats? I thought, bending down slightly to nudge the kids. "Sit still," I said under my breath. As I straightened up I saw a beautiful little girl sitting two rows up. She had a blue ribbon tying her golden ringlets back, and a blue dress laced with white. She couldn't have been older than five, and yet she was standing quietly between her parents, and I could just barely hear her singing along. None of my kids knew this song. So far as I knew, the only one I had gotten them to memorize was a song about Jonah being fish food. We weren't likely to be singing that.

Micah Hale called out another number, and the piano introduced it. "There's a call comes ringing o'er the restless wave; send the light, send the light! There are souls to rescue, there are souls to save; send the light, send the light!"

Jimmy was pulling on my skirt. "I need to go," he said.

David leaned past me and bent down. "Wait, Jimmy. I'll take you in a little bit."

Personally I didn't think that waiting was a good idea. Jimmy didn't have a very impressive track record of holding it, and I hadn't brought any extra clothes. But I kept my opinion to myself and tried to focus on the words in the hymnal. "Send the light, the blessed gospel light; let it shine from shore to shore..."

The song ended. Miss Palmer was playing soft chords, while Micah Hale was sweeping his eyes across the congregation. "The Lord is good," he declared, raising a hand in the air. "Does anyone have a testimony of His goodness?"

The piano chords continued. A stout little man near the front stood up, hooking his thumbs into his suspenders. "I have one, Mr. Hale," he said, "If I may. Not a month ago, there was some bad flooding all across the Meta area. We all know that. Thank the Lord no one was hurt."

Yes, I know, I thought. *I also know our translation manuscripts and notes were washed away. I don't want to hear about flooding.*

"One night after a day of pouring rain, our little son asked a question." He placed his hands on the shoulders of a round-faced boy. "He asked why God created gnats. They swarm about you and suck your blood, and that doesn't sound like a loving creator. And if God is so powerful, why make something so insignificant?

"First I explained to him that gnats didn't suck blood before the Fall, and we humans had brought that upon ourselves. But the second question stumped me. I sent him to bed and shortly after, my wife and I turned in."

He glanced from person to person with keen eyes. "Earlier that day a load of Bibles had arrived." There was a murmur of pride. These other missionaries hadn't done anything for this particular translation, but everybody felt they had a part in it. "They were still in their boxes in our shed. We were planning on a celebration when the rain let up.

"During the night, my wife woke up. A swarm of gnats were torturing the sleep right from her. At first she fought against them, and then she tried to ignore them. But folks, there's no ignoring the hand of God." His voice choked up and he pointed a finger in the air. "Finally she was forced to get out her hammock. And when she did, she looked out the window and saw the water licking our shed."

Everybody gasped, although we all knew the story must have a happy ending. After all, I thought, this was a testimony of God's goodness.

"She woke me up, and the two of us and our son rushed out to save the Bibles. We carried box after box up the hill, placing them beneath some bushes. The river washed our shed away and did some damage to the house, but nothing that can't be fixed. When the sun came out the next day, I looked at my son." His eyes filled with tears, and his voice was shaking. "I told him, 'son, God knows what he's doing. He always does.' My friends, God has a Master Plan." He thumped the back of the pew in front of him for extra emphasis.

Well, I didn't get any gnats, I thought.

There was another testimony from a grave, gray-haired woman, and then another song. "This is normally a Christmas song," Micah Hale said, "But it is good for any occasion, and a good reminder as to who is the ultimate ruler of this earth, and what joy that knowledge should fill us with."

"Joy to the world, the Lord has come; Let earth receive her King...

Let every heart prepare him room, and heaven and nature sing."

"Does anybody have any requests?" Micah Hale asked as the last notes died away. "If you don't get your request in, we will be singing more after the sermon and testimonials so don't fret."

"Higher Ground," Anthony said.

When I was younger, "Higher Ground" had always been my favorite hymn. Every Sunday I would scan the bulletin to see if "my" song had made it on the list; it had been my definition of a good church service. I believe it was the tune and the gusty way our congregation sang it that made me love it so much. But now, the words stirred my already confused feelings into chaos.

"I'm pressing on the upward way, new heights I'm gaining every day;

Still praying as I'm onward bound, Lord plant my feet on higher ground."

"David." My throat was dry, making my whisper sound more like croaking. "David, this was my favorite song."

"Jimmy, stop jumping," David hissed. "You can wait."

"No I can't," the boy groaned.

"You went at the Carter's house. You shouldn't have to go so soon."

"Lord lift me up and let me stand, by faith on Heaven's tableland;

A higher plane than I have found, Lord plant my feet on higher ground."

I had always assumed the song was talking specifically about Heaven as higher ground, but now I saw it in a new light – a haven on earth, almost. I sure wanted to be on higher ground. My mind flashed back to the rainstorm back in La Inez. The higher the ground was, the safer we were. My children could've drowned on the lower level. Suddenly I caught a glimpse of the river, as if I was in the jungle rather than a Catholic church. I was standing on a brink, gazing at the water that was eating away the earth. Rain splashed against my face. There was higher ground behind me, but I couldn't look away from the river. It was swallowing all that I thought was good and right.

I blinked, and I was back in the pew.

"My heart has no desire to stay where doubts arise and fears dismay;

Though some may dwell where those abound, my prayer, my aim, is higher ground."

But I couldn't just walk away from the river! It was getting higher, growing stronger. I had to keep my eyes on it. I could not walk away.

As a child my favorite verses had always been the last two, but I didn't want to hear them now. I took Jimmy's hand and walked down the aisle and out the door, shutting my mind and mentally calling these people names – cookie-cutter missionaries, roosting on imaginary hills of spiritual safety. Nobody was safe.

The outhouse was right behind the church. Jimmy ran in and I closed the door then leaned against it. I could still hear the singing.

I want to live above the world, though Satan's darts at me are hurled;

For faith has caught the joyful sound, the song of saints on higher ground."

I buried my face in my hands and cried. They were singing the chorus, but I couldn't hear them now, over the sound of my own despair. There was nothing I could do about the river. It washed everything away; it always had and it always would. Because that's what this earth is, a cycle of life after the Fall, with highs and lows, but in the end, everything is always washed away.

Suddenly I felt somebody touch my shoulder, and a feeling of strength returned that I hadn't felt in what seemed like forever. "Marilyn," said David, "Anthony said he has a gift for us at the compound. He's giving us a rocking chair someone else gave him." He laughed quietly, but then turned serious. "What's bothering you?"

"David, I'm sorry," I cried. "My focus should be on Him, only on Him, or I'm done for. Everything that happens – the good, the bad – I should see through His eyes and His Word, and not my own understanding. David, it doesn't matter that I'm living in a jungle – God has promised to guide us and watch over us. What matters is that we're gaining a greater insight into who He is."

He hugged me. "And now we've got a rocking chair," he whispered, a laugh in his voice.

The missionaries' singing drifted out the church.

I want to scale the utmost height, and catch a gleam of glory bright;

But still I'll pray till heav'n I've found, 'Lord, plant my feet on higher ground!'

Lord lift me up..."

"Are you all right, mama?" Jimmy stepped out of the outhouse, concern written over his little face.

"Yes, I'm all right," I laughed, reaching over and ruffling his hair. "Wash your hands, Jimmy, and we'll go inside."

He nodded, but I knew he was still uncertain as to why I was crying and laughing. A few moments later, we slipped back into our pew, just as the song ended. As somebody shared their testimony, I was silently repenting for my recent resentment and asking God for forgiveness, and asking for strength and direction.

"One more request," Micah Hale said, "And then we'll look into God's Word."

"Rock of Ages," Peter said. As the piano led us into the song, I noticed my children perk up. Dennis and Jimmy joined in, singing some of the words, humming through a couple ones they weren't sure about. Even Mary sang along.

We were a family, and God was our Father. Never had I felt such freedom. I had deserted the sinking sand I had stood on and I was safe. God was, and always had been, our rock.

15

Getting It Right

Time passed. One day, with my Spanish Bible tucked under my arm, I trudged down the path leading to a *maloka.* There were fewer than a dozen spread about in this section of jungle, each a few minutes walk away from each other. I was making the trek to visit one fifteen minutes (at the rate I walked) away from our home.

Several weeks before I had met a girl named Isabela when she was weaving baskets with Lucrecia. She had been heavily pregnant, and I estimated the baby must be born by now or would be very soon. While I held my Bible in one arm, my other carried a basket of soap and other supplies. If they wouldn't listen to me when I preached the Gospel, I would start with teaching them something they could easily understand. Perhaps I could gain their trust.

At last I reached a *maloka*. It was built on poles and raised above the ground like my own home; but instead of stairs it had a ladder, which was more practical for the Miyames to make. There were always a couple old people inside, and undoubtedly Isabela would be there resting. I hoisted myself up the ladder and stepped inside.

Light from outside filtered in through the woven palm leaf walls. The floor beneath me was split palm, which I knew was unbelievably strong, but it unnerved me the way it bounced. I was several feet in the air held up only by a floor crafted out of vegetation, and it wobbled with every step I took. This was one reason I avoided *maloka* visits. I shook my head and tried to focus on the job ahead of me.

"*¿Hola?*" I greeted in Spanish. A very old woman peered out at me. I continued in Spanish. "I don't know if you can understand me, but I'm looking for Isabela?" I repeated her name a few times, slowly and clearly.

I'm pretty sure the woman couldn't understand the language, but she knew the name. She pointed outside and then returned to her nap. I sighed, and climbed back outside. I walked around for a little bit, looking down different trails cutting into the jungle, trying to decipher which one would take me to the yuca fields. At last I chose the most worn path.

Only a minute or two later I found the women. I tripped over the vine-like leaves of a yuca, and nearly dropped my Bible. It seemed I was always clumsy around the Miyames. Straightening, I walked towards the closest woman. Lucrecia had pointed her out to me before; she was Isabela's mother.

"*Hola,* Anita," I greeted, hoping she knew Spanish. "*¿Donde está* Isabela?"

"Isabela?" Anita repeated. She waved towards her right. My eyes followed her gesture and landed on a crumpled figure beneath a tree. I turned back to the mother.

"Is she all right?"

"She is fine," Anita replied with a bit of a shrug. "She is only weary from work. We told her to rest in the *maloka* but she would not listen. Now she is resting there."

"Where's her baby?"

Anita shrugged.

Worried, I ran over to where the girl was lying. She was wide awake, staring up at the trees with silent brown eyes. I knelt beside her. "I hear you are not feeling well," I began. "How many nights since you had the baby?"

She raised a single finger. I raised my brows. "You should be in the *maloka*. I can help you go back."

She shook her head. I sighed.

"Where is your baby?"

She began to sit up, but I grabbed her and made her lie down again. She moistened her lips with her tongue and answered. "It was a weak girl. She is gone."

"I'm so sorry!" I exclaimed. Having had four children myself, the thought of a stillborn or premature infant death had always terrified me. I felt sick. "You must be..." I paused, looking for the right word in Spanish for *sad,* but then I finished my sentence using the Miyame word Lucrecia had taught me. "Do you have any other children?"

She shook her head. I sat beside her, stroking her dark hair. I wanted to let her know that somebody cared about her grief. What a tragic thing for a mother to lose a child, and the rest of her tribe didn't seem to care! I saw tears forming in Isabela's eyes. "If you want to cry, cry," I said. I wondered if anyone had ever said that to a bereaved Miyame girl before.

She looked at me in confusion, and then turned away. I set the basket beside her. She could still use some of the supplies. "This is a present, for you. Do you want me to show you what to do with these things?"

She shook her head. I sighed, rising to my feet. It was how it always happened; any conversation I had with a Miyame would wither and fade, I would go home, and start back at zero the next day. Gripping my Bible, I walked into the nearest clump of trees to hide the weariness on my face. *God, help me find a way to get through to them. They don't trust me, and they think they're safer ignoring me.*

After a few moments of walking and praying, I realized I had strayed far from the clearing. Not wanting to get lost, I turned to go back the way I came. But a small sound caught my attention. It sounded like a cough; the weak cough of a newborn baby. I glanced around, looking for the source of the noise.

Setting my Bible down, I peered into a bush. My heart skipped a beat as my eyes landed on a tiny, naked newborn, lying in a pile of dead leaves. With quivering hands I picked her up and held her against me. She was beautiful, and whoever had left her out here to die was going to answer for it.

Picking up my Bible, I stormed back to where the women were working. As usual they kept on with their work, but this time I wasn't going to be ignored. Gripping the baby tightly with my legs braced apart, I shouted, louder than any Miyame had heard me before. "Who left this child in the jungle?"

I believe they were surprised that one of the background-noise missionaries was yelling. But I was indignant and fuming, and my voice should've been the least of their worries. "Tell me, now! This moment! Who is this child's mother?"

Most of the Miyames didn't understand Spanish and were whispering to others, asking for translation. A murmur spread through the group as everybody repeated what I had said. Isabela was sitting up, looking at me with frightened eyes. I took a step forward.

"Cecilia," I said, calling out a woman I had met before. "Whose baby is this?"

"It is one of ours," she admitted, but I already knew that. She was side-stepping the question. "But it is weak and cursed."

"Anita," I tried again. There was a heavy trace of suspicion in my voice. "Whose baby?"

Anita was the only one not ruffled. She looked me in the eyes coolly. "It is Isabela's, my daughter," she answered. "It is as good as dead."

I turned towards Isabela. Now she was crying.

"Isabela," I said, my anger still hot, "Did you leave your baby to die?"

"We do not want a cursed girl," she whimpered. "I will have another baby in a year, I am sure."

"She's not cursed," I argued, "Have you asked your shaman?" The shaman was their medicine-man and unlike some, he was relatively laid-back about curses, and seemed more interested in finding ways to cure skin irritations with jungle plants. Most of the superstitions in the tribe came from the people themselves.

Isabela shook her head and cowered. "My mother told me to leave it," she said. "She was with me."

"Put her back where she came from," Anita said indifferently, picking up her hoe. "We have no need for another girl."

Many of the women had already gone back to work. Would they ignore me about this too? Even in the warm air the baby was shivering in my arms. I held her tight. Every life deserved to be fought for.

"Isabela, this is your child," I cried. "She is beautiful, look at her!"

Isabela cowered.

This was one thing I couldn't just walk away from. "All of you, listen to me now!" I shouted. "Do you give your children snakes to play with? Do you feed them poison? No, that would be murder! But you are killing this baby. She is one of you, she is one of your children. You have no proof that she's cursed. If she were grown already, would you kill her?"

"Are you preaching, sis?"

I spun around. My brother was standing behind me, his hands in his pockets.

"Steven," I gasped. I switched to English. "What are you doing here?"

"I thought Linda told you I was coming," he said with a shrug.

"Well of course she did, but – I mean, I thought you wouldn't be here until next week. How did you find me?"

"With how you were yelling, it was easy," he answered. I rolled my eyes, and he smiled slightly. "I met your friend Peter at the house, and he brought me up to that longhouse down the trail from here. We ran into a native and Peter started talking in Spanish, which of course I don't understand. So I came down without him to attend your fiery sermon. What was the text?"

"It's great to see you. I would hug you," I said, "But my hands are rather full." Really, I mostly wanted to slap him. But I put on a smile, and then glanced awkwardly from the Miyames to my brother.

"I will take her," Isabela exclaimed suddenly, staggering to her feet. "She is mine."

With a sigh of relief I handed the baby to her. "Now go rest at the *maloka*," I instructed in a muddle of Spanish and English. "And take care of her."

Isabela nodded and hurried off. The rest of the women had returned to work as if nothing had happened. I stood gazing at them for a few moments, until Steven touched my shoulder. I turned around. "It's been a year and a half since I've seen you," he said. "Can we have a proper hello?"

I flung my arms around him. "Steven, I'm sorry. I'm just so distracted right now. These people were trying to kill a baby, and I got angry... oh, never mind. Let's go find Peter."

As we walked down the trail, my mind flooded with a million questions I wanted to ask him. Was Mom doing all right? Was Dad still in good health? How was Meredith? Did they still celebrate Christmas together? But instead I just soaked up his presence. He was wearing a collared shirt and a black jacket (not what I would recommend for jungle wear), and I could see his favorite gold watch on his wrist. It was like he was wearing America – it was imprinted in his mind and it seeped out. His accent was northwestern, and even the smell of his hair gel could only be found back home.

"You're awfully quiet," he remarked. "You a little winded after your spiel to those women?"

I smiled in spite of myself. "I guess I'm just glad to see you."

"How's life been? Is it always as... invigorating as that speech you were giving?"

"Steven, forget about my yelling. I was angry and lost my temper. You couldn't understand what I was saying, anyway."

"Yes, I can see you've learned Spanish. You speak it rather well."

I gave a lopsided smile. "If you knew the language you might say differently."

"Have you hit any exciting milestones yet?" Steven asked. "I don't know how you missionaries do things down here, but I suppose you've got some goal."

"We haven't been here that long," I said. *God, help me not sound defensive.* "We're still getting used to the people and their culture."

We both went silent for a few moments. At last he spoke again. "I chatted with that German pilot on the way here. He said there's been some bad flooding, and you nearly lost your kids."

"God had His hand of protection over them," I answered, trying to stay calm this time.

He nodded. "I also heard that Peter was bitten by a venomous snake. Are snakebites very common here?"

"We have some antivenin in the house now if you're worried," I answered.

He shrugged and shook his head. As we stepped into the clearing with the *maloka,* we were greeted by Peter. "Hello, Marilyn," he said. "Are we headed back to the house now?"

"Yes," I answered. "We need to find David and tell him Steven's home. We need to find Lucrecia and pick up my kids, too. Steven,

David went fishing with Chief Jaime. They might be back home before we are."

We began the walk back to the house, and Steven and I began chatting about home. He told me that Meredith had finally made up her mind to attend nursing school, and was finishing her first year. Our cousin James had gotten married to that sweet girl from Roseburg, and Uncle Lenny had finally gotten that television set he had been talking about for years.

The fifteen-minute walk didn't last long enough. We came out into the clearing, and I saw Jake's airplane sitting on the runway. Half a dozen Miyame men and a couple women were gathered around the chief's house, and I spotted my children with them. I walked across the strip and joined the group.

"*Hola,* Marilyn," Lucrecia greeted, stepping toward me.

I returned the greeting. "Where is David?"

"He is inside with the chief," she answered.

I nodded. "It looks like the men caught a lot of fish."

Each of the men around us was holding a tough string with one or two large fish strung up. "Yes," Lucrecia said, her dark eyes sparkling. "They caught many. We are waiting for the chief to come out and divide it evenly among the families."

The Miyames were always sharing. If a group of men caught fish, everybody was sent home with some, no matter how many the individual had caught. Their method was to look out for the entire tribe as long as everybody at least tried to help.

"This is my brother," I said. "Steven Turner."

Lucrecia's eyes widened. "You have a brother?"

I smiled. "Yes. I have a sister too, but she lives far away."

Lucrecia turned to Steven. "Where are you from?"

Steven glanced at me. "Translation?"

"She's asking where you came from," I explained.

"Well, go ahead and tell her I'm visiting from the States."

"Lucrecia, he lives in a different country."

Before I could explain further, Mary ran up to me. "Mama," she whined, "Dennis did it."

That was about the limit of her vocabulary, but it was usually all that was needed. "Dennis, what did you do to your sister?" I asked.

The little boy pointed to a fish lying on a large, razor-edged leaf. "She was biting me, so I tried to make her smell the fish to stop."

"Marilyn," Steven said, smiling slightly, "Could you introduce me to these two? I believe I met one of them, when he was much smaller."

"Oh!" I exclaimed. "Dennis, say hello to your uncle."

"Hello," he said in English, then in Spanish, "¿Mamá, *quién es él?*"

Dennis almost always spoke Spanish, and it was the only language Mary knew. With great relief and satisfaction I realized their fight had been in a language Steven couldn't understand. "He's my brother," I said, "And I want you to speak in English."

"Do they only know Spanish?" Steven asked, looking slightly muddled.

"They know English," I said, "At least the three older ones do. It's more like a second language to them, though. But I practice with them nearly every day. English is school to them."

"I'm Uncle Steven," he said, holding his hand out to Dennis. "What is your name?"

"I'm Dennis. That's my sister Mary. She's mean, she was biting me..."

"Dennis!" I interrupted. So much for teaching them English. "Steven, would you like to meet the older two? They should remember you."

I led him past a group of Miyame men, chatting in their strange gurgle. Sadie was sitting on a piece of wood, reading aloud a new book Anthony and Joyce had given her. Jimmy sat on the ground, fiddling with a piece of grass, listening intently.

"'*Cuanto cuesta la entrada hoy al jardín?*'" Sadie was reading.

I interrupted her. "Children, do you remember Uncle Steven?"

They both looked up, and a look of immediate recognition crossed Sadie's face. Jimmy needed a few more moments, but then his eyes lit up. "You lived in that big house with the blue blanket," he exclaimed, "and the popcorn, and the little red stool!"

"Funny the things you remember," I laughed.

"Sadie, you're quite the reader!" Steven commented. "Of course, I haven't the slightest idea of what you were saying, but I'm sure you were doing a good job."

"It's a story about a man visiting all the sights in Bogotá," explained Sadie.

"He's trying to get into the botanical garden, and then he'll climb Monserrate!" Jimmy said excitedly. "Sadie, read that part."

"Not right now," I said. "Sadie, why don't you put the book away. Then you can help me make dinner."

16

An Open Door

My brother and I walked up to the house, followed by Peter and the kids. I wanted to tell David that Steven was here, but I decided that if he was talking to the chief it was best not to interrupt him. I grabbed Mary's hand and helped her up the porch steps.

"Did Peter show you around the house?" I asked Steven.

He shook his head. "No, we headed straight out to find you."

"Well, here it is!" I wanted to gesture with a wave of pride, but instead I shifted nervously. I loved my brother too much for him to be disappointed with where I lived and what I did. He only nodded and glanced over the cracks in the walls.

"This is the porch," Jimmy said. It was obvious, but I was thankful he was breaking the awkward silence. "At night-time it's Peter's bedroom. He sleeps in that hammock."

Steven brows rose slightly. "Do you really sleep out here?"

Peter was standing at the foot of the porch steps. "Yes, I do," he answered.

"Even when it's raining?"

"The porch is covered, so yes. But we're almost done building my house."

There was more to the story, but even though time had passed since the office shed was washed away, none of us liked to talk about it.

"Hmm." Steven followed us through the door. Inside we found Jake Perry, lounging on a chair with his feet propped up on the stove, a cup of coffee in his hands.

"Hallo, Marilyn," he said, lifting his cup towards us as a way of greeting. "Kara insisted I not fly home till I woke up a little. I found some coffee on the stove. I hope you don't mind that I helped myself to it."

"Isn't it cold?" I asked, lifting up the pot. "I can warm it up."

"Naw, it's better this way," he answered. He yawned. "Mind giving Kara a call and telling her I'm about to head back? She's expecting me for dinner."

I went over to the radio and Steven followed. "How many books of the Bible have you translated?" he asked.

"La Inez to La Casa," I said before turning to my brother. "There was a missionary here before us, and he had a few small books completed. Unfortunately he didn't make any effort to insure them with copies, and they were all lost in a flood. We're working on James right now."

Kara's sweet voice interrupted. "La Inez, I'm here."

"Hello Kara! My brother is talking to me, so I apologize for any interruptions..."

"Marilyn," Steven persisted, "Why did the other missionary leave? Did you ever find that out?"

I pressed my lips together and gazed at the radio, trying to think of an answer. But no, I hadn't the slightest idea of why Jim Warden had left. Nobody had ever told me. *Could it be tied to what he did to the*

Miyames? I had almost forgotten that Jim Warden had refused to help the chief's son, and the child had consequently died.

"Warden wasn't the best for the job," I said at last. I let go of the transmitter button to see if Kara was still there.

"Why do you say that?" her sweet voice asked.

I had forgotten she could hear me. I pressed the button again. "Kara, I'm talking about Jim Warden. You remember him." I tried to laugh. "He left the job half-finished."

"I remember him," she answered. "He was our neighbor for longer than you and David have been. Why do you say he wasn't fit for the job?"

"Don't you remember the way he treated people? He tried to talk us down and tell us we couldn't convert anybody. And he outright lied to David by making up a bunch of stories about his father." I shook my head. "Kara, David's father was an honorable man. Warden said he died in a shameful fight."

"There's always going to be people hard to get along with, Marilyn. Sometimes they're wrong, but sometimes they're right."

I straightened up indignantly. "You're not saying Warden could possibly..."

"I'm not talking specifically about anyone. But truth doesn't always come in the nicest or purest form. We've got to melt the dross from the gold, and perhaps with Warden there's more of one than the other. But you can't condemn him, especially without knowing the full story."

Jake cleared his throat. "Kara, *liebling,* I'm headed home."

"You sound exhausted," she said.

He shrugged. "I'll go find a bucket of water to dunk my head in. That always works."

"All right, see you soon. Goodbye, Marilyn. La Casa out."

Before I could speak, both Kara and Jake were gone.

Peter sat at the desk and began sifting through papers. Steven sat down at the edge of the bed, his mouth lopsided and one brow above the other, surveying the house. Trying to forget Kara's words, I grabbed my pot and pan and set them on the stove.

"Marilyn," Peter said. He straightened and then withered with hesitation, but tried again. "Marilyn, you didn't actually know Weldon Cole, did you?"

"Maybe not," I snapped, "But I know David's mother and sister, and they knew him."

"Of course," he backtracked. "But what about everyone else who knew Weldon? I know you asked Anthony, and he didn't know him. But what if Warden really did..."

I gritted my teeth, and then forced myself to take a deep breath. "I don't think this is necessary to discuss, Peter. Perhaps you can go see if David is coming back yet."

"Of course." He hurriedly shuffled his papers together. My eyes on my pot, I listened to the door creak open and shut and he was gone.

I squared my shoulders and began measuring rice. Trying to sound composed, I asked, "Sadie, do you remember the box of books Anthony gave us? Could you set them on the shelf? Dennis, Jimmy, could you set the plates on the table?"

"Where's the box?" Sadie asked, wandering about the room in a tight circle. "I can't find it."

How could we lose anything in this size of a house? *Besides one sock from each pair,* I thought with a tight smile. That was something that could be lost anywhere, anytime. I turned my focus back to the problem at hand. "Boys, do you know where it is?"

Jimmy was grabbing the plates off the shelf, while Dennis was standing beside him, holding a toy truck we had bought him in Bogotá. Nodding, they stepped over to where Steven was sitting. "Can you get up?" Jimmy asked. Steven stood and Jimmy flipped up the covers. Together the boys pulled a large box out from the crates that made up our bed.

"Who put that there?" I demanded, slightly embarrassed.

"Dad did," Jimmy offered, "Because he broke the crate that was here."

"How did he break it?"

"He was trying to hit a frog with your frying pan," explained Jimmy, "'Cause he said it was poisonous. He got it, too."

I had just poured eggs into the pan. Hurriedly I asked, "Did he wash it?"

"No, but he only used the bottom," Dennis said.

Sadie pried open the box and tugged out a large book. Staggering towards the shelf, she scanned the cover. "John Calvin... Insti... I can't read the English."

Bindings scraped together and papers rustled as Jimmy heaved another out. "This book's written by a Catholic," he announced, "Anthony said so."

"This book is falling apart," Dennis said, lifting up a handful of pages.

"These books have gone through many hands. That's what Anthony said." Sadie lifted Calvin's Institutes and plunked them onto the shelf. "I don't know how Daddy's going to sleep tonight. We just pulled his side of the bed apart."

The door opened and Jake peeked his head in. Water was dripping from his yellow hair, and his blue eyes had lost their lethargic glaze. "I'm heading out now," he informed us, "Enjoy your brother's visit." He nodded towards Steven, gave a friendly wave towards the kids and then shut the door.

Steven folded his arms and leaned against the wall. I watched him shake his head slowly, his eyes darting about our house. My heart sank like a stone in water.

"What sort of economy do they have down here?" Steven asked. He began pacing the room, as if it were fuel for his rapid fire of questions. "What do you do for school, for your kids? What do you eat?"

"My kids are fine," I said, forcing myself to speak calmly. "We teach them ourselves for now, and perhaps they can go to the school in Mosbaya when they're older. As for food..."

"What happens if you stay on the mission field until Sadie's a teenager? A six-year-old should be looking forward to a life with peers and friends."

"She can make friends here," I said. "By being here, she gets to witness a missionary's life firsthand, which I think she'll look back on as an amazing experience."

Steven shook his head. "You can't do that to a teenage girl, Marilyn."

"Well, she's not a teenager right now, is she?"

"You've got to think ahead, Marilyn, like I've been telling you all along," Steven argued. "Ever since you first told me about your harebrained scheme to convert a random jungle tribe, I've tried to bring your attention to your children. They won't be kids forever."

I sighed and gave my eggs a stir. There was a moment of silence.

"Do they get enough to eat?" Steven asked at length.

I slammed the spatula into the pan. "Of course, Steven," I snapped. "You never asked me that in the States, did you? Do you think I've changed as a mother? You used to help me feed bananas to Sadie and Jimmy. I do the same thing with Mary now. It's not as different as you might imagine."

"Except you get your bananas shipped in here by a German pilot who has to dunk his head in water to stay awake," Steven pointed out. "I want confirmation, Marilyn, that there is a reason why you're here – a real, tangible reason that I can see with my own eyes!"

There were loud, thumping footsteps coming from the porch, and then the door burst open and David was suddenly inside. "Come quick, Marilyn!" he shouted. "The chief wants all three of us! He's making an official apology!"

"A what?" I asked, blankly.

David ran in and grabbed my hands. His blue eyes were sparkling. "He wants us here now. He is desperate to hear what we have to say, simply desperate! He's agreed we speak the truth!"

"And he's apologizing for not believing us before?"

"There's more to it than that!" David took a step back and subconsciously sat down on the edge of the bed, but the covers gave way beneath him and he crashed onto the floor. "Who moved the box?" He cried, scrambling out of the mess of blankets. "I had a box here, who moved it?"

"We did," Sadie said. "I'm sorry. Mama wanted the books."

"It doesn't matter." He wrapped Sadie up in a big hug. "God worked a miracle today, Sadie!"

"What's the apology?" I asked.

David turned to me again. "Chief Jaime said he's been telling his people to ignore us. He thought it would intimidate us, and we'd leave without him actually telling us to – he felt he owed us something for saving his life that one time. But we stuck with them, Marilyn, and I spent the whole day telling him the plan of salvation while we were fishing, and he wants to learn more! He wants us here!"

My heart was pumping with excitement. "That's amazing, David!"

David scooped up Mary and gave her a tight squeeze. "Jaime says all the men will be back soon. Arturo will help us continue our translation, and Jaime says he wants to help too! He's very fluent in Spanish. He's very smart. He's invited us to a tribal event they're having later this week, and he wants me to give a little speech after he does. God is opening doors, one by one!"

God, thank you! I prayed silently. My heart was nearly bursting with joy. "Let's go see him," I said, hurriedly taking the pan off the stove. "I want to thank him for accepting us."

David set Mary down, and gave a little jump of surprise. "Steven! I didn't know you were here. Welcome to our home! Come meet the chief!" And with that, David was out the door.

Everything went quiet. I could hear cicadas buzzing (our version of crickets). Steven gazed at the floor silently, while I set the eggs on the table. Finally I glanced at him. "I think there is a reason we're here," I said quietly. "Are we square now? Can we agree to disagree?"

"Never do that, Marilyn," Steven said. "Stick to your beliefs and respect others', but never agree."

I began to wonder what they taught in law school.

Moments later, Steven and I found ourselves in Chief Jaime's hut. David was holding his Spanish Bible and Peter was standing beside him.

"I know a lot of this book already," the chief was saying as we entered. "The first missionary, Warden, read it to me. I liked the words, but I did not like the man. But since then, I have heard this book read on my radio. The radio has spoken about this book and how it is important that true followers of God tell others of Him."

"You waited to see some confirmation," David said. "This Book claims to change lives, but you waited until I had proved it. But you've waited long enough! The Gospel has confirmation on the very meaning of your existence! We're both sinners, and until we're perfect, we can't live with a perfect God, who is the Chief of all chiefs and the Creator of the world."

"I have put it off for a very long time now," Jaime said earnestly, "But I will not any more. I have thought it through. This is God's book, and if He is the greatest Chief of all, and if He has a message for us I want to hear it. I have known this since Warden came. Now I want to understand it."

At Steven's request, Peter was quietly translating the conversation. I was lost in thought. *This sounds familiar... I know God's message, but I learn day by day that I haven't fully understood or applied it. Jaime knows there's something missing in his heart, and he wants to fill that space. God, help me overcome any pride or trust in my own reason and logic that may be hindering me from You. You have given all the confirmation I could ever need.*

The next morning dawned bright and dry. I was poring over schoolwork with Sadie, trying to help her understand her grammar. The other kids were playing on the runway with the chief's little boy, Juan. David was spending the day at Jaime's house, and he had taken Steven with him.

I heard the door swing open quickly followed by Peter's excited voice. "The men are back, Marilyn," he exclaimed. "Arturo's with David and the chief already!"

Before I could answer, Peter rattled on. "Arturo said that he repaid his debt and took nothing more. He's going to help us translate every day, he said, and you should've seen how determined he looked! He'll get the Bible translated, even if he has to do it himself!"

He disappeared, leaving Sadie and me alone. I closed my eyes and took a moment to let my head clear. *It really is worth it all,* I thought. *After mournful silence comes joyful noise, after night comes day...*

"This sentence sounds right to me, Mama," Sadie said desperately, interrupting my philosophizing. "Why are stringy sentences bad?"

About an hour later, Steven came in silently and sat at the edge of the bed. Sadie had gone outside to play, and I was setting lunch on the table, enough for Arturo and Jaime if they wanted to come over. I continued quietly, letting my brother think. He was gazing at the ceiling, lost in thought.

"Marilyn," he said suddenly, "Do you think I'm a little stubborn sometimes?"

I glanced at him. He had filled his hair with gel again, even though we had told him several times that morning it wouldn't do any good in La Inez's setting and climate. His hair was falling into his face. "Yes, just a little," I answered.

"Do you suppose, sis, that I can be stubborn with myself?"

If anybody could, it would be him. "We're all stubborn with ourselves sometimes."

His eyes slowly traveled across the room, as if soaking up the fibers of the structure that held our lives. "I see you and David, and I see that chief, and I know something good is happening. But I don't want to accept it."

"You're a lot like Jaime," I said. "You've got the brains to know what's right, but brains sometimes keep us from opening up our hearts."

He rose to his feet. "Before I came out here, I had it all planned out, what I was going to say to you – the lectures, the scolding, the persuading. But since the moment I flew into this little world of yours, I've realized it's not what I imagined at all. You're not what I envisioned you would become, you're just David and Marilyn."

I laughed. "But what about this tribe we're trying to convert? This makeshift house we live in? The pilot who dunks his head in water to stay awake?"

"It is very different," he said, "A different way of living. But you're doing it for the same reason you did things in America, and I see that now. It's... hard to explain."

Surveying the ready meal, I sank into a chair and grabbed a book. "You don't need to, Steven. I understand."

I flipped open to where I had left off reading the night before. It was a compilation of some of the writings of Ann Judson, given to us by Anthony. *"When we recollect that Jesus has commanded His disciples to carry the gospel to all nations, and promised to be with them to the end of the world, and that God has promised to give the nations to His Son for an inheritance, we are encouraged to make a beginning, though in the midst of discouragement, and to leave it to Him to grant success in His own time and way."* Ann Judson could sure pack a punch in one breath. And I had spent the whole morning teaching Sadie to not use stringy sentences.

17

The Whole Story

Two days after Steven left came the appointed day for the tribal event. I got the children ready, while David and Peter prepared the chicken we were bringing. We had never been to a tribal event before, but Arturo had promised to take us there and explain how they did things.

We made it outside and met up with Arturo and Lucrecia. "How is the food served at an event like this?" asked David in Spanish.

"Everybody brings something," Arturo explained, "And everybody gets something."

"Arturo, do you know how the chief knows Spanish?" I asked. "Several of the younger people know it from time spent in Mosbaya at the Catholic school, but didn't Jaime say he never went?"

Arturo nodded. "I spent time with missionaries in Villavicencio, and I learned Spanish there. Jaime is my uncle, and he has a mind that wants to learn. I taught him the language. We were hoping to learn English next."

"God supplied us with a pair of gifted linguists," laughed David. "Marilyn, isn't that amazing?"

I had to admit, it was beyond amazing. Arturo and Jaime were a tremendous force when it came to translation, which we had discovered during the past couple days.

"I asked God to send my tribe hope," Arturo said sincerely. "Even before I knew who He was, I remember watching Jaime speak to the spirits, asking to understand. Then I went to Villavicencio and Warden brought the Bible here to La Inez."

The Miyames had never heard of God before Warden came, yet God had always been there, preparing their hearts and setting the stage. It was like a painting an artist draws of his childhood home, or a portrait of himself; he weaves colors and shapes together with a piece of his own soul. God had drawn his master plan on His canvas, and although a Miyame may not understand the significance, there was no missing the picture.

We arrived at the arranged party grounds. Some of the families were claiming trees and stringing up their hammocks since they intended to stay all night, sleeping when they needed it. We approached the chief and Lucrecia presented her dish to him. He set it with the rest of the food, and then I stepped forward and handed him the chicken.

"*Hola,* Jaime," I greeted. "Thank you for allowing us to come."

He nodded. "You will hear many songs that speak of our culture and our traditions. Also, you will get to know my people better. You will tell them about God's Word."

"Thank you, Jaime," I smiled.

We sat down around the area marked for a bonfire. A few old men were already singing old, sad-sounding songs, but the real singing would begin when it got dark. I watched the young men light a match and apply it to their kindling. Gently they blew the small flame. I glanced at Arturo.

"Where did they get the matches from?"

"The rubber barons," he answered. "We are accepting more from them than we have for many years. We also buy matches in Mosbaya."

"How far away is Mosbaya?" David asked.

"Two days' journey," Arturo answered. "Some of the children go to the Catholic boarding school there."

The first few attempts at lighting the fire had failed. One of the young men was lighting another match. "They're going through those things rather quickly," I observed.

Arturo shrugged. "They have plenty. They got theirs from the rubber men." His eyes wandered towards the sky. "Today we have the choice to work for them or not. It was not always this way."

"I heard that the rubber barons held this land in a reign of terror," David said. "Warden mentioned it, but he didn't detail very much."

"My Grandfather lived in those days," Arturo said, gesturing towards an old, wrinkled man sitting at the other side of the fire. "He is one of the few to survive."

The old man was gently humming a tune that seemed as ancient and melancholy as he was. The song sent a shiver down my spine. "How much do you know about how the rubber barons treated your people?" I asked curiously.

"I know all the stories," he answered. "I have heard them from the survivors, and I spoke of it with the missionaries at Villavicencio. They knew much about the suffering my people went through." He began tearing a blade of grass in his hands down the middle. "They told me that for every ton of latex shipped from this country, the blood of seven natives had been spilt."

"The rubber barons of today are evil," Lucrecia said, "But they are nothing to the ones of the past. They were slave masters, and forced every one of us they found to work for them."

Arturo nodded. "And those who resisted were tortured and killed. Those who became too ill to work were beaten. Any who did not collect enough rubber were used to provide entertainment or target practice for the white men. They would tie a sack on a native's head, set it on fire, and cast bets as to whether he could find the river on time or not."

Sadie and Jimmy were listening with wide eyes. I think I felt sicker than they did. I could tell by the heavy look in Arturo's russet eyes that his people had suffered much more vivid and cruel torture than he would even describe, or that we could bear to hear.

"Once a man misinformed the rubber hunters about what a gathering of a nearby tribe was doing," Arturo continued in a low voice. "He told the hunters that the tribe was preparing to attack them. This tribe was actually having a festive dance, like this." He waved his hand towards the men, women and children gathered about us, bustling about the food, chattering with each other, and playing games.

"When the rubber hunters approached the tribespeople, they offered them some of their festival food as a sign of peace. The rubber men shot them, and then burned down the *maloka* nearby where many of them were gathered." The pieces of grass dropped from his hands. "Over a hundred died that day."

"Arturo," Lucrecia said, "The stories only grow darker. Our friends have heard enough."

Arturo bowed his head in agreement. "Since those days, our people have tried to live quietly, but we have turned to witchcraft and fear to forget the pain of the past. This tribe, and all the others cannot forget the past so easily. The rubber barons today are watched by the government; but when a man is once bitten by a snake, can he have dealings with the snake again without fear, even if it has no poison? How are we to know the poison is truly gone?"

He looked at us earnestly, the fear of his tribe mirrored in his eyes.

"Marilyn!" Anita walked up, ending the dark conversation. She was carrying a plump baby in her arms. "Look at my daughter's little girl. Lucrecia asked me to show her to you, and then bring her back for food and rest."

"She's beautiful!" I exclaimed, rising and running my fingers through the baby's dark hair.

"She is the only baby that does not scream all the time," she said proudly. "And the healthiest. I do not think she can ever get sick! She looks like her grandmother."

Her behavior had been very different when this baby was young and weak, I noted.

"Mama, can Dennis and I go play with our friend?" Jimmy asked, tugging on my skirt.

"Who, Juan?" I asked. Juan was a shy little boy, who was currently hiding behind the legs of his older brother Misael, a young man of nearly twenty. "Yes, you may. Stay where I can see you."

As they ran off, I thought of Chief Jaime's family. Of his three sons, only Misael and Juan were still living; the middle child had died when Warden refused to help. My fingers clenched. Jim Warden had gotten away with far too much.

"Marilyn, Arturo wants to go to the States someday," David said, tugging me back into their conversation.

"The States?" I exclaimed. "You're very ambitious, Arturo, but if I know you, you'll get there. What do you plan to do there?"

"I am not sure yet," he said, "But perhaps God wants me there. Ever since I was young I have heard Him speak to me as the Creator of all I saw; I did not understand His voice, until I met the missionaries in Villavicencio. I did not accept His voice until your family came. But now I hear Him. I cannot grasp all that He says, but I know He is with me and wants to use me."

I squeezed David's hand as Arturo continued to ramble, his eyes fixed on the fire.

"Perhaps I will tell your people about mine. I will tell them about our history, and the rubber barons, and our superstitions, and how we are without hope. The ones who know God's peace will want to help us. The ones who don't will learn that they must find it."

The next morning, I sat down to write a letter to my parents. Anthony had asked us if we had any mail we wanted to send, and I knew Jake was coming in with supplies that day.

Dear Mom and Dad,

I can only write on this small piece of paper because Anthony is paying for its delivery, and I do not want it to weigh more than necessary. But my heart is burdened to tell you about the first convert in La Inez. Not for our sake, that you would have a better opinion of us as messengers, but for yours, that you would understand what a mission truly is.

Arturo is a young man who helps us with translation work. God has gifted him with the talents of words and language. He is planning on learning English. Arturo and his wife Lucrecia were raised with the stories of the torture and death that ravaged his family long before they were born. They have watched their people slowly recover, like a crushed flower trying to bloom again.

Through this, Arturo met God. He says he has always known there must be a Creator. During his search for peace, he has traveled through several villages and towns and met missionaries in another city. There they told him more of what he had been looking for. And at the right moment in his life, David and I stumbled into his own village.

I know you wanted to hear news of my little ones, but I sincerely believe this is a story to share. Through Arturo and his uncle Jaime, we have been accepted as part of this tribe, and now David works on translation with the two of them, my sons play with Miyame boys, and I have shown the women how to care for their babies. If it hadn't been for Arturo and Lucrecia, none of this would have been possible. But David and I did very little for his salvation. Which brings me to the most important truth about missions: we don't save people. God does.

Your loving daughter,
Marilyn Turner Cole

On the bottom strip of the paper I crammed in a *P.S.* I paused, reconsidering what I had been intending on putting down. But something in my mind urged me to tell my parents of the man whom I had made my personal thorn in my side.

The missionary who was here before us, Warden, made a mess of his job that was hard for us to get past. He also talks badly about David's family. Please pray I do not lose my temper next time his name is mentioned.

There wasn't room for any more. I could hear Jake's airplane coming in, so I quickly folded the letter and raced outside.

"Good morning, Jake!" I greeted as he climbed out.

"Hallo, Marilyn," he replied. His blue eyes were shifting, and his face was strangely pale. I hadn't talked with him since that day he had been drinking our cold coffee, and I wondered if he was getting sick.

"David is behind the house," I said slowly, "He can help you refuel."

He abruptly grabbed my arm. "Marilyn," he said, "I can't stop thinking about what you said to Kara the other day. Please don't talk badly about Jim Warden."

I pulled away. "Maybe you don't know him like I do."

"Does that give you an excuse to talk about him like you do?" Jake said. "He was a good friend of mine, and I know he can be stubborn and opinionated. But you don't have to take offense at everything he says."

"I'm not only offended," I answered, "I'm disgusted. Arturo told us about what happened when the chief's son was dying."

Jake's face blanched.

"Yes, I know the story," I continued, my chin held high. "Jaime asked Warden to bring you in to take the little boy to a doctor. Warden refused to call for help."

"Oh, Marilyn," Jake said, with a pained expression, "So this is why you hate him! It's my fault the chief's son died and only mine. Jim did call me, but I had taken my plane to Bogotá for minor repairs. Please, leave it to God to judge."

He turned away, rubbing his head agitatedly. I watched him disappear behind the house, and slowly I looked at the letter in my hands. *Perhaps there was a misunderstanding, but God, Warden still did talk bad about David's family!* Ephesians 4:32 flew into my head: "And be ye kind one to another, tenderhearted, forgiving one another, even as God for Christ's sake hath forgiven you." Slowly I unfolded my letter. Another verse came to mind.

"Judge not, and ye shall not be judged: condemn not, and ye shall not be condemned: forgive, and ye shall be forgiven."

God, the gold and the dross, all of it – help me leave it to you. Deliberately, I tore off the bottom strip with my *PS* and I ripped it to shreds.

18

The Visitor

Several weeks after our first tribal event, Jake arrived early in the morning with his usual supplies. Kara had come with him and was giving my kids a medical checkup. While Jake and Peter were unloading, I was on the front porch with David and Arturo setting up a compact cassette player Anthony had sent to us. We were pushing in cassettes and attempting to get it to work.

Peter had been helping Jake, but he stopped for a moment to watch us. "Is that the new cassette player?"

David took the letter. "Yes, it is. We're trying to figure out how to use it."

"We should order some bluegrass cassettes," suggested Peter. "That's what I always listened to back in the States."

Jake approached us, a heavy crate in his arms. Jaime, the chief, was trailing behind him. "Here are the food goods," he announced. "Before I go, I'm going to take Jaime for a little flight."

"I have been on a plane before, but I was sick and did not enjoy it much. This time I want to look at my house from above it," Jaime said somberly, but I could sense hidden excitement. "What is that you have, David? Is it a radio?"

"It's the cassette player I told you about," David answered. "Remember? I showed it to you in a catalogue."

Jake shook his head. "I never have enough money for what I look at in catalogues. Like an Aeronca, with a set of dandy floats."

Jaime looked confused, but David always surprised me with how much he knew about everything, like Aeroncas. "It's a type of seaplane," he told the chief. "I can imagine it being out of your budget, Jake."

Jake set the crate down and straightened up. "Just a few more things I need to take out, and then we're up in the air. Perhaps someday, Jaime, you'll be flying a Cruiser on your own."

A low hum suddenly met our ears. Everybody quieted, listening. "Sounds like an airplane," David said, a split-second before the sound was joined by sight. A dark grey Piper Pacer swooped low over our clearing, disappeared, and then returned, diving into the trees towards our runway.

"Knucklehead!" Jake shouted, racing towards the runway and yelling as if the pilot could hear him. "You aren't landing on this runway if you know what's good for you!"

The pilot seemed to not know what was good for him. Relentlessly he plunged onto our narrow landing strip, hitting it with a bounce and breezing down it briskly. Jake's plane was still sitting at the end of the runway; the intruding Pacer tried to slow down to avoid hitting it, but its speed proved to be an unconquerable force. At the last moment the plane turned sharply, avoiding Jake's Cruiser by an inch and landing itself in the ruts beside the runway.

"Clumsy nutter!" Jake fumed. "He nearly took out my plane!"

"Who is that?" I asked, as we all stepped off the porch. "Jake, do you recognize this plane?"

"I haven't the slightest idea who it is," he replied, "And I know every pilot in the area."

Curious, we stood and watched as two men clambered out. One had a darker skin tone and was dressed in camouflage fatigues, while the other was a pasty white color with blonde hair. He was dressed in jeans and a t-shirt, and a silver cross hung over his chest on a necklace.

"Morning," the second man called. The first stayed behind, pulling fuel out of the backseat to fill the plane.

Jake was silently fuming and I was eyeing the strangers with distrust, but David greeted them with his usual smile. "Good morning," he said. "I'm David."

"Cole, yes, I know," the man said, crossing the last stretch of runway. He held out his hand. "Brett Simpson."

"Nice to meet you, Brett," David said, shaking it. "What brings you out here?"

"You, actually." He turned towards the plane and shouted, "Camilo, bring my satchel, will you?" in Spanish before turning back to us. "I'm here representing the MLA. We want you back in the States."

"What?" David and I said in unison. His was more in shock, while mine was indignation.

Brett held his hands up, palms outward. "Hold your horses. I'm talking about furlough, that's all. I've got a letter from your sister Linda explaining why you're getting it earlier than expected, and we have the details all worked out. You're coming back with me. All expenses paid. It's pretty much a family vacation."

"This is... unexpected," David said. "I wish you would've sent us a letter in advance. When are we supposed to leave?"

Brett glanced at the runway. "Day after tomorrow."

My mind was spinning. A trip back to the States would be nice, of course, but it was a time-consuming, expensive ordeal that we weren't expecting for a few years. Linda's work at the MLA was always conducted in a sensible, painstaking way, and I couldn't picture her waking up one morning and deciding to send this blonde man with a necklace out to pick us up on a last-minute furlough.

But Brett Simpson was standing before us, living proof that something along those lines had happened.

Camilo, the Colombian in fatigues, ran up with a satchel that Brett swung over his shoulder. I suddenly remembered my manners. "Would you like to step onto the porch?" I asked. Kara was still in the house doing checkups with the kids, and I figured the porch was cleaner anyway. "And can I get you anything?"

"Water would be nice, thank you," Brett said, following David onto the porch. We had no furniture there, but Brett sat down on the wood planks without a fuss. By now we were used to sitting on the ground, but it was strange to me to see three Americans - Brett, my husband, and Peter - sitting in the Miyames' traditional squat.

When I came back outside with the water, Jake was leaning against the railing, close enough to be part of the conversation but I could see his eyes following the Colombian as he refueled his plane. I handed Brett the water, and he thanked me before turning to David. "Questions? Concerns?" he asked, amiably enough.

I noticed that David had the satchel in his lap, and he and Peter were evaluating the contents. David had Linda's letter in his hand. "The MLA wants me to speak to their students?" he asked, and I could tell he was overwhelmed by the strain in his voice. "Linda knows I'm a terrible public speaker."

"It doesn't have to be a speech," Brett said smoothly. "We'll help you come up with a presentation. If you have pictures we can put them on the projector. Your wife can share something, Peter can share something. Also, I think they plan to have Jim Warden share your presentation, since he served in the same village and all."

Jake's eyes snapped away from the runway. My heart froze. "We're supposed to speak to the students together?" I asked, being careful to keep any emotion from my voice.

Brett nodded. "That reminds me. While I'm down here, I'm supposed to ask some questions: a survey, of sorts. If at all possible, I'd like to speak to each one of you individually. I'll ask you questions to ensure that no one down here has been performing against the MLA's mission statement, so we in the States have a better idea of what's going on down here. Each interview will be private, of course."

"So we can complain about each other?" David asked, frowning.

Brett shook his head. "Hopefully you'll only have good things to say about each other, and it'll be a brief, straightforward question, but unless we do these things, how are we to know that there isn't some malpractice going on down here? Anyway, the reason I remembered is because I'm also supposed to ask about your experience with Jim Warden. Be thinking of your answers."

If I had been asked a year ago to evaluate Jim Warden, I would already have my answer. He was cruel, he was a liar, and his mission ideals were everything I stood against. But now, I wasn't so sure.

"This is insane," Peter said, looking up from the satchel. "Why are you carrying around every single ticket it'll take us to get back to the States? And all of this cash, and coins?" To prove his point, he held up dollar bills mixed with pesos, letting them fall from his hands and drift back into the bag.

"That bag is all you need to get back home. You're going straight to Colorado, Peter, while the Coles get a week in Washington," Brett explained. "I see you found Linda's letter."

"Yes, but she says barely anything," David said, "Except to follow your instructions."

"I know all of this is sudden, but it'll make more sense down the line," Brett promised. "Now, could I have a few minutes with Peter?"

Wordlessly, David set aside the satchel and followed me into the house. Through the cracks in the walls I could see Brett and Peter walking towards the river, talking quietly. Jake came inside with us and sat by the window.

"How are things going?" Kara asked. She was on the floor, trying to wrangle Dennis still to measure his height.

"Fine, but strange," David said honestly. "Brett Simpson from the MLA is here. We're supposed to leave on furlough, day after tomorrow."

"Kara," Jake said, "Didn't we get a letter saying that ours was coming up?"

She nodded thoughtfully. "Yes, we did. Ours is supposed to come first, and they certainly shouldn't be so close together. Where is Brett Simpson now?"

"He's talking to Peter," David said. "He wants to ask us questions about our experience with Jim Warden. I don't get that, either. I didn't know him long, but I suppose he was all right."

"We knew him for several years," Kara reflected. "He wasn't perfect, but he was a good friend."

"He said some terrible things, though," I said half-heartedly. "He said we'd have trouble with Jaime. He called him a stubborn man who didn't want to admit that he was a guilty sinner in need of punishment."

"And you know what? He was right," Kara said gently. "Sometimes we get bad impressions of people, Marilyn, but you didn't know him long enough to pass judgment."

I sighed in frustration. "Why does it matter if I give a favorable report of him or not? We don't need him. He's retired and not coming back anytime soon."

"He lied about my father," David said through his teeth. "He said he died in a fight."

"But I've heard that, too," Jake said. "I honestly thought the same thing."

"Sometimes we hurt ourselves by not giving others a chance," Kara said, looking directly at me. "It doesn't seem like Warden can affect your mission anymore, but we don't know what God has planned for him. Just be sure to be honest about him with Brett. And in order for that to happen, you need to be honest with yourselves."

Peter opened the door. "Marilyn, Brett would like to talk to you."

I stepped outside and met him on the porch. He smiled at me. "I'm not a marriage counsellor, so don't worry, I won't ask you anything about David. Do you have any concerns about the other missionaries in your area, including but not limited to the Carters, the Perrys, and Futterman? If you don't have any concerns that could hinder the MLA's mission, please say 'pass' and we won't even have this conversation."

"Pass," I said.

"See? It's that simple," he said encouragingly. "Now, I know you only spent a few months with Warden, but I imagine he spent a lot of time with your family. Unless his behaviors raise any concerns that could hinder MLA's mission, please say pass."

"Pass," I said.

"Wonderful. We rely entirely on our missionaries' reports of each other to make good calls. If you'd voiced any concerns, we would have had to open an investigation, and that takes time and money. Sometimes we have to remove the missionary."

My mind brought up Warden's sudden retirement. "Has that ever happened to anyone in this area?" I asked.

He shook his head. "Not Colombia," he said. "Now if you'll excuse me, I'd like to talk to David."

19

In The States

In June of 1976, we stepped into an old, vaguely familiar realm. Cars honked, street lights glared in the late spring rain, and advertisements for everything imaginable played on TVs and radios. Holding onto our bewildered children tightly, we exited the airport and climbed into Olivia Cole's car. She drove us through the town we used to know. We had traveled first by Jake's Cruiser, then Anthony's pickup, then a steam engine, then a boat and finally by passenger plane to reach Washington State.

She took us straight to a diner where Linda was waiting for us. We hurried inside to get out of the rain. After the three years we had spent in La Inez, we should've been indifferent to rain; but I had always hated the drizzling, cold gray rain that characterized Washington. A rainforest deluge was better than this.

Peter and Brett had split from us in a layover and were on their way to Colorado. In a week we would meet up with them at MLA's linguistic camp. So it was David, Sadie, Jimmy, Dennis, baby Mary and me.

Olivia and I chatted with the children while David and Linda ordered us some food. The two were arguing over who was going to pay for the meal. Their family did this every time they got together: aunts, uncles, grandparents, cousins, every generation would argue over who was going to pay and try to give each other money. If somebody offered to pay in my family tree, my relatives would accept it easily. Because of that, offering to pay was a rare occurrence.

At last they got it settled and we got our food. David prayed and we dug in. I watched my children devour everything set before them, and I dreaded the stomach aches I knew were coming. Our stomachs were not used to this kind of diet.

Olivia and Linda drove us to their house and we all went to bed early. The next morning, the kids found old bicycles in the garage and insisted we take them outside. On my way out, Mary on my hip, I caught sight of an old rocking chair in the corner of the living room that I hadn't noticed before. It was made of old knothole-spotted wood, with a red and white checkered cushion thrown on top.

"I thought you would have gotten rid of that chair by now, Olivia," I commented.

She smiled, shaking her head. "I was going to send it to the dump, but I just couldn't. Don't sit on it, or it might fall apart. I've been hoping David would come back soon enough to fix it."

"In Colombia he told me how much he missed that chair," I laughed. "He'll be more than happy to fix it up."

Olivia stayed inside to fix us lunch, and Linda stayed in her office to get some work done. David and I went outside with the kids, two bikes and a wagon. It was a quiet, tidy neighborhood, and before we had moved to Colombia we had taken many walks up and down these streets.

Birds were chirping delicately, a stark contrast to the noisy birds we were used to. I called out advice to Jimmy every so often, who had only ridden a bike once at the Carter's compound. Sadie was completely comfortable on hers; she kept pedalling ahead of us, looping in circles on the street until we caught up.

We came to a stretch with a sudden ditch on one side of the road. A car was driving by, so David pulled the wagon with Dennis and Mary in it to the side, keeping a tight hold on it so it wouldn't slide into the ditch. Sadie and Jimmy joined us, letting the car pass by, and though the ditch wasn't that deep I did lunge forward to keep Jimmy's bike from going over the edge.

"Daddy, careful!" Dennis yelled, staring at the ditch as if it were the Grand Canyon. "We're gonna fall!"

"I've got you, son, you're safe," David assured him.

Not convinced, Dennis scrambled to his feet and toppled out of the wagon, away from the ditch. I had to grab him to keep him from running into the road. "You're okay," I told him soothingly, "it's just a little ditch."

"I thought the wagon was gonna fall," he whined. "I don't wanna fall over the edge."

"You're not going to fall," Jimmy huffed. "The wagon's perfectly safe. It's not even close."

"You know, Dennis, you weren't scared because you saw the ditch," I said, brushing dirt off his clothes. "It's because earlier, when we were on the road, you looked around and thought you were safe."

"Was I not safe, Mama?"

"You were - both times. But it's not about what's around you, like a ditch or a road. It's about who's pulling the wagon. Daddy won't let you fall." I kissed his hair. "It's the same with God. Sometimes we get scared, but God holds us in the scary places the same way He holds us in the safe places."

He nodded gravely and climbed back into the wagon. David smiled at me. "I wasn't expecting you to sermonize him back in."

"It was a good opportunity to teach him something I've been learning," I shrugged.

He put his arm around my shoulders and squeezed.

Our week with David's family passed quickly. Olivia and Linda came with us to Colorado, where the kids and I were given a hotel and a day to settle in. David was immediately hustled away to meet with Peter and Jim Warden and plan a presentation. The next day we joined him at the MLA mission conference held in the MLA campus.

The conference was in the auditorium. The seats were the kind that you pull down to sit on, and when you stand, they fold back up. My children found them utterly delightful and kept trying to fold them up while sitting on them and sandwich themselves between the seat and the backrest. I sat there and wondered what logical reason there could be to design such a chair. Olivia and Linda had come with us, but they were sitting in the very back.

The place was full of MLA students as well as people who had come specifically for the conference. I hadn't seen Warden yet, but I knew David was with him somewhere. I could see Peter, setting up a 35 mm slide projector so we could share some pictures.

David slipped back into our row right as the conference began. One of the higher-ups of the Association - I think he was Peter's father or uncle, but I wasn't sure - shared a brief message from God's Word, and then led everyone in a few songs. He then introduced Jim Warden and asked him to come forward.

Warden still had his dark beard and his eyes were as narrow as I remembered. Besides that, he honestly didn't look as menacing as I had come to picture him. He gave a very straightforward account of his ten years in Colombia, and what it was like to build a house and runway with nobody to help but Jake Perry. He also mentioned how though he never got very far with the tribespeople, he did encourage them to send their children to school, which had raised the number of Spanish-speaking people in the village.

When it came time for him to invite our family to the stage, he looked directly at us. "Allow me to introduce the people who took over my position," he said. "In '73, I was diagnosed with a condition that mandated my immediate return to the states. I was unhappy with the news, and I must confess it was more because of my pride than anything else. I had set out for the mission field with visions of grandeur, and I was leaving with nothing. No progress, no miracles, no stories worth telling. Passing my failure over to be fixed by people who I don't even agree with on many things was difficult."

He shrugged, looking away from us to the audience at large. "But I have learned that it's God that saves people, not us, so why should I consider myself better or worse than my fellow believer? I trained the Cole family for life in Colombia and then took my leave. I am in excellent health now, so no need for concern in that regard. I have been refreshed by my stay here and I hope to return to active work before long, Lord willing. I am going to ask David Cole and his family to come to the stage, so he can share with you the admirable work they have been doing for the Miyames. David?" He held out the microphone.

He stepped off the stage and we stepped on. As David talked about the Miyames, my eyes followed Warden to his seat. *He's not perfect, God,* I prayed, *but help me forgive him for that.*

I tuned in to what David was saying just as he was quoting 1 Timothy. "It truly is a faithful saying, 'and worthy of all acceptation, that Christ Jesus came into the world to save sinners.' Thank the Lord for that."

He talked for only a few minutes, and then Peter took over. He turned on the projector and showed several pictures, explaining each and occasionally sharing a story or anecdote. After the presentation was over, everyone sang a few more songs and then we were dismissed. Another missionary family from Uganda would be there the following day to speak, so the audience was reminded to come again tomorrow.

"How have you been, Peter?" I asked as he joined our family in the lobby. "Did you get to see your family?"

He shook his head. "My mom just moved to Boston, so she isn't in the area anymore. Dad's here, though. He wants me to stay here and take over her job."

"Is that something you're considering?" David asked.

"Not right now," he shrugged. "A few years from now, maybe it'd be nice to live here in Colorado and work with the students. But for now I'd rather be on the mission field."

"Your presentation was wonderful," Olivia praised, joining our little group. "Your father would be so proud, David, if he could see you now."

It was the first time my father-in-law had been mentioned during our visit, and I froze. I could tell by the look on David's face that he was going to ask the question I was too scared to hear the answer to. He looked at me, and I tried to make my expression say *no, no, not now! Do you really need to know?* But he either misread my expression or ignored it, since the next thing he said was the dreaded question that had followed him since our move to Colombia.

"Ma, I'm going to ask you an honest question, and I'd appreciate an honest answer. How did dad die?"

For a moment she looked confused. "It was in Colombia, son, you know that."

"He got sick, yes, you told me," David said. "But Ma, people in Colombia have a different story. The story down there is that he died in a fight."

I would have approached this entire conversation differently, but my husband wasn't one for tact or for beating around the bush. Olivia brushed the hair out of baby Mary's face, a distant look in her eye. "We can discuss this later, in private."

"But can't we discuss it now?" David pleaded earnestly. "You got to choose what story I believed my entire life. Don't I get a chance to choose now?"

Linda Cole walked up at that moment, and from the look on her face she had overheard part of the conversation. "Tell him," she said simply. "With what's in store for him today, he needs to know."

What's in store for him? I thought, panicking.

Olivia thought for a moment, and then turned to her son. "I didn't lie to you," she said gently. "He was very sick when he died. There was a guerilla outbreak in the area, and there were snipers trying to use our village for cover. Your father was foolish and thought he could intervene and make them go away. He was shot before he had a chance to speak."

Sadie and Jimmy were listening wide-eyed, while Dennis and Mary were more interested in digging through my purse for snacks. I watched a gamut of emotions pass over David's face: loss, betrayal, confusion, and anger. At last he gave his mother a small smile. "It's okay," he said, giving her a side-hug. "I wish you had told me, but it's okay."

If somebody in my family lied about something (which honestly happened regularly), the drama would never end. I still don't understand how the Coles can just hug it out and walk away. Olivia and David were both a little teary-eyed, but it was nothing compared to what I would have expected.

Your father was shot, David, I told him mentally. *And your mother lied about it! Don't you want to know why? You started this conversation against my recommendation, you might as well finish it!*

Linda, I had come to learn, made a little more sense than her mother and brother. "David, you were a baby when it happened but I was plenty old enough to understand," she explained. "I was angry with Dad for years. We had been advised to flee the country, but he had chosen to stay and risk our family for the sake of the Gospel, and it got him killed and left us fatherless. As I grew older I accepted his decision, but my anger was why Ma changed the story for you."

"I wouldn't have been angry," David insisted. "Why would I be angry that my dad risked his life on the mission field?"

"It's not the right decision every time," Linda warned.

"It was for him," Olivia said with calm assurance.

Linda shook her head. "Ma, watch their kids for a bit. David, Marilyn, I need you upstairs with me. Peter, you too."

Her tone boded no good. I had been wondering if we were in trouble. We weren't even supposed to be in the States right now; why bring us back unless we had done something wrong? Olivia gave us a sad smile that did nothing to reassure me and took the children.

20

Saying Farewell

I didn't feel any better about the situation when Brett Simpson met us at the top of the stairs. His blonde hair was swept across his forehead, and he had the same cross on a chain around his neck. This time he was accompanied by a girl with short, dark hair.

"Good job on the presentation," he said. "This is my fianceé, Emma. Emma, as you know this is David and Marilyn Cole and Peter Futterman. If you could join me in the meeting room, we can get started."

We followed him inside. There was a table covered with scattered papers and unlit candles, with Peter's father and Jim Warden sitting opposite each other. Brett waved at the chairs with a welcoming smile and we sat down. Linda took the head of the table, with Brett and Emma beside her.

"Let's cut to the chase," Linda said. "David, we pulled you out of Colombia in response to the increasing violence in the country. Your family can't go back."

David jumped to his feet, nearly knocking over his chair. "You told me we were coming to the States for a conference!" he exclaimed, his voice shaking with betrayal. "Why is it always okay to lie to me?"

"Sit down," she said sharply, and he slumped back into his seat. "Getting your family out of danger was our first priority. There are still options, but we wanted to speak to you face to face before we decided anything."

"What violence are you even talking about?" I asked. "The rubber barons have never caused us any trouble, and the Miyames are definitely not about to hurt us."

"We're talking about guerilla warfare," Brett spoke up. "My father is a foreign relations agent and generally works with the Colombian government. He says that the U.S. will most likely begin drawing out all of its citizens before long."

"There are a lot of us down there, and we aren't afraid," I argued. "The Perrys, the Carters, Micah Hale, all those people at the Bogotá conference... I can't imagine all of them being rooted out. It's impossible."

"It's very, very, possible and undoubtedly likely," Brett said seriously. "Colombia is reportedly the most violent country in the world. Maybe the chaos hasn't reached your neck of the woods, but it will. The drug cartels are growing. The country is heading towards war, and it'll be of the bloodiest, cruelest kind."

"We want to keep working down there, we really do," Linda said. "But there comes a point where courage is just stupidity. I pray things will blow over soon, but until that happens we have to adjust to the times we're living in."

David looked as shaken as I felt. "We didn't even say goodbye to people," he said. "We only said we'd be back. We didn't finish anything. They don't have a Bible, they don't have a church. We did nothing."

"You did the best you could," Brett said, and he sounded sincere.

"I feel for you guys, I really do. You've been in my prayers for quite a while."

"You said we had options," David said, turning to Linda. "You said you wanted to talk to us face to face about options."

She nodded. "We're not pulling everyone out just yet," she said. "The MLA board has approved two men to continue working in La Inez until things get worse."

"So there's a chance I can go back?" Peter asked, hesitantly.

"A very high chance," she assured him. "Jim Warden is present because he has requested permission to go back, but David, we're giving you first dibs. It's your mission."

Everyone looked at David, who was doing a good impersonation of a deer in headlights. "I... I can't take Marilyn? Or, or, the kids?" he stuttered, and Linda shook her head. He looked at me and then back at his sister. "Give me a moment, will you?" he asked before jumping up. He grabbed my hand and dragged me out the room.

The moment the door shut behind us he grabbed me by the shoulders. "Tell me what to do," he begged. "It's up to you, Marilyn. I don't know what to do."

My mind was racing and my heart was thumping. There was so much to process. David might be leaving me alone with the kids. Or Warden might be taking our place. I might never go back to Colombia. All of the possibilities made me sick.

"Let's talk about it, okay?" I said, trying to curb his panic and stifling my own. "If you went back, I could live with your mother. The MLA would still support me and the kids, right?"

"Right, yes," he said.

"So that's feasible. But what are the cons?"

"I can't leave you!" he said. "I have to go back, Marilyn, but I've got a family. Linda can't really expect me to make this choice!"

He was crying again. Never in my wildest imaginations did I expect my life as a missionary to end like this: comforting my husband in an empty hallway. I hugged him and he clung to me, and I wished I was as good at making people feel better as the Coles always seemed to be.

"You're right, sweetie, it's an impossible choice," I said, trying my best. "But we have to make it, right? Linda's only doing what she thinks is right. Knowing how your father died really puts some perspective to it, don't you think?"

He pulled away, looking me in the eye. "What would you do if I died the same way?" he asked, and my heart stopped. "If I went back and I died, what would you do?"

"I'd thank God for considering us worthy to suffer for Him," I said, trying to convince myself. The words felt hollow.

"Can something be right for one person, and wrong for another?" he asked in anguish. "God gave me a family, Marilyn, long before he called me to the mission field. What kind of man would I be if I left you?"

"Tell them to send Warden," I said, and I knew I was begging. "Your father did what he felt called to do, so shouldn't you do the same, even if that means staying here? Stay with me and the kids, David. Don't go."

"I'll stay. Unless God says differently, I'll stay," he said.

I hugged him. "Can you pray?" I asked.

Even though we knew the others were waiting with us, we took our time talking to God. David prayed and I listened, and the minutes ticked by. Slowly we both relaxed. I understand now why they call it peace 'that passes all understanding.' I can't explain it, but we had peace.

We opened the door and went back inside. Everyone was still in their seats, talking quietly, though they stopped as we came in. David and I sat down.

"I'm staying here," David said simply. "I don't feel it's right for me to go."

Linda looked at Warden. "Jim?"

"I'd be willing to go with Peter to La Inez," he affirmed with a nod of his head.

"Thank you, everyone, for meeting today," Linda said, standing up. "I know that most of you were not expecting things to change so suddenly, and I'm truly sorry. I need to go keep this conference going, but I'll be around if anyone has any thoughts or questions."

As she walked out, the man who I thought was Peter's father turned to us. "I'm Ken Futterman," he said, "And I've got a job opening here at the campus. Care to give it a try?"

I remembered Peter saying that his mother had just retired from her position. From what I understood, she was in charge of accounting and financing, which, as much as I love David, I can't say he was good at. David seemed to share my hesitation. "What sort of job?"

"I've got a couple, actually. Peter's mother just retired, but I also need a new head of maintenance and construction. I don't know what your skillset is outside of linguistics, so I'm not sure if either of those are feasible."

"I used to do construction," he said eagerly. "Framing, usually."

"I want a new hangar on the south end of the campus," Mr. Futterman said, adjusting his glasses. "As part of helping indigenous people around the world to be less reliant on our missionaries, we want to have the ability to teach them to fly. We're starting a new flight program here for our students so we'll have more pilots in the field to teach them."

"I can do that," David assured him.

The next few weeks were a whirlwind as we changed our home address, our diet, our goals and our mindsets. David was indeed hired by the campus. We bought a little house not far away, and Olivia decided to sell her home in Washington and move in with us.

In August of 1976 we pulled up to the Denver airport to drop off Peter Futterman. Olivia stayed behind to watch the children, so it was just the three of us. The plains around us were brown and dry, while a sharp wind was keeping the summer temperature down. We walked with Peter into the airport terminal, all three of us pretending to smile.

Once inside, David stood on his toes to see over the crowd of people. "I see Jim Warden," he announced. "It looks like he's waiting for you."

Peter nodded, adjusting his glasses. "I guess this is goodbye."

"Tell everyone we said hello," I told him, "and that we'll miss them."

"Try to get along with Jim Warden," David said anxiously. "I know he's a little thick-headed sometimes, but you're both down there for a cause bigger than yourselves. Don't let him ruin it for you. Same thing with Chief Jaime, don't let his stubbornness throw you off. And stay updated with what's going on politically down there. Keep in contact with the Carters as much as possible."

"David, I think he can handle it," I said.

He sighed. "I know, I just can't help but worry." He took Peter's hand and shook it firmly. "Come see us sometime. We'll keep you in our prayers."

"I appreciate it," he said. We watched as he shouldered his bag and walked away, wandering through the crowded terminal to find Jim Warden.

The sense of loss that settled over us was something I never want to feel again. After all of the years we had spent preparing for mission work, and the years we had spent on the field, it was excruciating to watch two men walk across the terminal to take our place.

David spoke and summed it up well. "It feels like we've lost the place. La Inez, I mean," he said.

"It was never really ours, was it?" I asked. "If staying here is God's plan for us, He'll be with us the same way he was in Colombia."

"Makes me think of my dad's favorite verse," David said.

"'*Whether we live, we live unto the Lord; and whether we die, we die unto the Lord: whether we live therefore, or die, we are the Lord's.*' You know, I'm glad missionaries get to believe everything we teach."

I smiled. "So am I."

He grabbed my hand. "Let's go home, Marilyn," he said.

"Nothing in my hands I bring: simply to Thy cross I cling."

"And be ye kind one to another, tenderhearted, forgiving one another, even as God for Christ's sake hath forgiven you." Ephesians 4:32

About the Author

At a young age, **A. L. Helland** would captivate her ten siblings on long car drives with tales full of adventure, laughter and purpose. An avid reader, she once read an 800 page classic as a twelve-year-old just to prove she could. Nowadays, she has been writing for over ten years, sharing her talents in a wide range of styles and genres, and is the author of the *Paradox* series. She is the founder of Willamina Studios, where she helps to provide wholesome entertainment through books, music, audio dramas and more.

www.ingramcontent.com/pod-product-compliance
Lightning Source LLC
Chambersburg PA
CBHW070616310726
48982CB00001B/97